SPECIAL MESSAGE TO READERS

THE ULVERSCROFT FOUNDATION
(registered UK charity number 264873)

was established in 1972 to provide funds for research, diagnosis and treatment of eye diseases. Examples of major projects funded by the Ulverscroft Foundation are:-

- The Children's Eye Unit at Moorfields Eye Hospital, London
- The Ulverscroft Children's Eye Unit at Great Ormond Street Hospital for Sick Children
- Funding research into eye diseases and treatment at the Department of Ophthalmology, University of Leicester
- The Ulverscroft Vision Research Group, Institute of Child Health
- Twin operating theatres at the Western Ophthalmic Hospital, London
- The Chair of Ophthalmology at the Royal Australian College of Ophthalmologists

You can help further the work of the Foundation by making a donation or leaving a legacy. Every contribution is gratefully received. If you would like to help support the Foundation or require further information, please contact:

THE ULVERSCROFT FOUNDATION
The Green, Bradgate Road, Anstey
Leicester LE7 7FU, England
Tel: (0116) 236 4325

website: www.foundation.ulverscroft.com

CASTLE OF FLOWERS

When an opportunity arises to catalogue ex-model Astra Dempsey's famed fashion collection, Evie Quinta jumps at the chance. She hopes she'll be able to find out what happened to her father years ago, when the powerful Vicente family forced him to flee his native land of Portugal — something he never talks about; and Astra had been married to a Vicente. But once Evie arrives, it isn't long before she realises she's stumbled upon a bigger secret — one that Felipe Pereira, Astra's grandson, seems determined to protect at all costs . . .

MARGARET MOUNSDON

◆

CASTLE OF FLOWERS

Complete and Unabridged

LINFORD
Leicester

First published in Great Britain in 2018

First Linford Edition
published 2019

A catalogue record for this book is available
from the British Library.

ISBN 978–1–4448–4293–7

Published by
F. A. Thorpe (Publishing)
Anstey, Leicestershire

Set by Words & Graphics Ltd.
Anstey, Leicestershire
Printed and bound in Great Britain by
T. J. International Ltd., Padstow, Cornwall

This book is printed on acid-free paper

Disturbing Memories

'You'll pay for this.'

Her father's threat echoed in Evie's ears as she stood in front of the stout oak door of the Castelo de Flores. Francisco Quinta was the mildest of men. What had happened all those years ago to turn him against the Vicentes? Evie had only been a toddler but the memory of his anger had stayed with her over the years.

Taking a deep breath, she straightened her shoulders. She wasn't here to rake up the past, she was here to work. She tugged at the wrought-iron bell pull. It echoed down the corridor but no-one came to answer it. She tugged again with renewed vigour, wishing her taxi driver hadn't been so quick to drive off once she'd paid the fare.

A car sped by on the dusty track of a road, the driver hooting at an unfortunate cat who had chosen that moment to stroll across his path. With an outraged yowl the animal disappeared in a cloud of dust as the car hurtled on down the hill, radio blaring, tyres squealing.

Despite its grand name the castelo appeared to be little more than an art nouveau villa decorated with the blue and white patterned tiles that were a distinctive characteristic of the area. From what Evie knew of the Vicente family they would consider living in a villa to be beneath them. Nothing less than a castelo would befit their status.

Her lips curved into a wry smile. Were they so stuck in the past that they didn't realise class distinction had died out years ago? Or had her father been right? They didn't know about the problems of ordinary folk and what was more, they didn't care.

Before Evie could give the matter further thought she heard the sound of bolts being slid back. The door swung open to reveal a woman with a distinctly unwelcoming face who spoke brusquely.

'Do you speak English?' Evie's knowledge of Portuguese suddenly deserted her.

'*Inglê? Não.*' The woman looked Evie up and down. '*Paparazzo?*' she sneered.

'No.' Evie was vehement in her denial but that didn't stop the woman closing the door in her face.

Evie stepped back in shock and stumbled over her suitcase. What exactly was going on here? She rifled through her bag to double check the details Lesli had given her before she left home.

'Good luck, kid,' had been her parting words. 'I hear they're a tricky bunch. Knock 'em dead.'

Evie never quite understood how Lesli operated her agency, but she was a good friend who would never have allowed Evie to be left stranded in the middle of nowhere.

Evie squinted at the typewritten print.

'The Castle Of Flowers, Marina, Southern Portugal.' She read the address out loud then inspected the dusty nameplate on the sun-baked wall. 'Well, I'm definitely in the right place.'

Attached to the details was the transcript of a brief communication received from Astra Dempsey saying she was looking forward to meeting Evie Quinta at the end of the week. Evie bit her lip in frustration. This was taking the recluse thing a bit too far.

Evie's white T-shirt stuck to her back as the relentless April sun beat down from an azure sky. A butterfly darted in and out of a lavender bush, its wings a vivid orange contrast to the vibrant purple flowers. The castelo was aptly named. Everywhere was a riot of colour.

Dragging her mobile out of the pocket of her jeans Evie re-checked the telephone number then keyed it into her phone. In the distance she could hear it ringing. Growing more annoyed by the minute, Evie stepped back to look up at the façade of the house.

The windows were shuttered against

the fierce afternoon sun. There was no way she could gain access from the front. It was then she noticed a side door tucked away behind a trailing bougain-villea bush. Feeling like a trespasser, Evie pushed the door open, peered round and raised her voice.

'Hello? Anyone home?'

Again she was met with a wall of silence. Trundling her suitcase behind her she followed the path round to the back of the house. The view from the terrace robbed her of breath. She dropped the handle of her suitcase. Now she understood.

From its imposing position on the headland the castelo looked out over the bay. Yachts bobbed in the harbour but Evie's eyes were drawn to the magnificent rockery boasting a display of flowers, the like of which she had never seen before.

The smell evoked memories buried deep in her past. She inhaled the tang of scented thyme and was instantly drawn back to the days of her childhood when she had lived with her parents in their tiny farmhouse further down the village.

She remembered how her father used to love working outside and Evie would toddle along behind him on chubby legs as he walked up and down the vines inspecting the foliage for signs of rot or infestation.

She swallowed the rising lump of emotion clogging her throat. The vine-yard had been his life. Evie steadied herself against a garden statue, her hand on her chest as she willed her breathing to return to normal.

She must remember why she was here. Her father, a dignified man, would not have wanted his daughter to rake up the past.

All the same, it was part of her heritage and something neither her father, nor her mother, would talk about. When Evie had tried raising the matter with her mother she had shaken her head.

'Your father has moved on with his

life,' she said, 'and we must do the same.'

Reluctantly, Evie drew her eyes away from the view and back to the castelo. The doors to the terrace were open and a dropped sunhat on top of a magazine indicated that someone had recently been sitting there.

A disturbance caught the corner of Evie's eye. She could hear the snip of secateurs and see the glint of sun on a wheelbarrow.

'Hello?' she called out again.

'Good heavens, you made me jump.'

An elderly lady poked her head through a juniper bush. She was wearing a similar straw hat to the one discarded on the terrace. Her mesmerising eyes were a deep green velvet colour and although her hair was now soft white and her face bore evidence of her years Evie would have recognised her anywhere.

The last time Evie had seen her was in a photograph. She was standing by a swimming pool, dressed in a scarlet evening dress, wearing a diamond tiara and a pearl choker, her hair carefully disarranged, her eye make-up smudged. A recumbent tiger appeared to be looking at her in adoration. Her special smile signified mystery, sophistication and a sense of being. The photo epitomised a generation.

The woman smiled at Evie.

'Hello, I'm Astra Dempsey.'

A Shock for Felipe

'Astra?'

Evie heard a male voice calling her name. Astra made a face.

'Felipe, my grandson. I suppose there isn't time to hide?'

'Er, no.' Evie faltered over her reply. 'I don't think there is.'

'He is so bossy,' Astra confided, 'just because my heart had a little flutter recently. I'm supposed to rest in the afternoon. I keep telling him I'm not an invalid but you know what men are like. They never listen.'

'There you are.' A lithe dark-haired man strode towards them. 'Who's this?' He fixed his dark brown eyes on Evie.

'I don't know,' Astra admitted.

'Then would you please leave?'

'Darling, you're not being very polite to our guest.'

'She isn't a guest. You don't even

know her name.'

'He's right, you know.' Astra's green velvet eyes twinkled with amusement. 'May we know who you are?'

'My name is Evie Quinta.'

'I knew you'd have a pretty name.' Astra's face lit up. 'You're too lovely to have an ugly one. Don't you agree, Felipe?'

Felipe continued to glare at Evie who decided it was time to get down to business.

'I rang the bell but the woman who answered it closed the door in my face.'

'That'll be Catherine.' Astra betrayed no surprise. 'She's very protective.'

'*Avó*, why don't you sit down on the terrace and leave this to me?'

'You're as bad as Catherine,' Astra grumbled. 'Evie, when you have a grandson do not let him dominate you.'

Just then, Catherine approached, casting no more than a sour glance at Evie.

'It is time for your siesta,' she told Astra.

'Perhaps I am a little tired,' Astra

admitted, stifling a yawn. 'Will I see you at dinner, Evie?' she asked.

'Miss Quinta is not staying,' Felipe replied.

'Nonsense, of course she's staying. I invited her. Come along, Catherine, you can carry these.' She loaded Catherine down with her garden tools and strolled across the stubby lawn back to the terrace.

'I am here by your grandmother's invitation,' Evie insisted.

'That I find difficult to believe.'

Felipe crossed his arms and waited patiently while Evie rummaged in her bag for the crumpled copy of Lesli's note.

'Here.' Evie thrust the piece of paper under his nose.

Felipe scanned the note, his frown deepening as the meaning became clear.

'My grandmother wants you to catalogue her fashion collection?'

'Yes.'

'Why was I not told about this?'

'That's something you will have to

take up with your grandmother.'

Felipe hesitated.

'Is that your suitcase?' he asked, pointing towards Evie's luggage.

'What?' She swivelled round. 'Yes, sorry. I abandoned it because I was struck by the view. Isn't it lovely?'

Evie felt her spirits rise. Surely someone who lived in such a beautiful place couldn't be a grump all the time? One look at the expression on Felipe's face suggested she might be wrong.

'What I think of the view is neither here nor there. I am going to have to ask you to leave.'

'What?' Evie's voice rose in disbelief.

'Of course I will pay any expenses you have incurred and I'm sorry your time has been wasted.'

'Now listen here, Mr — ?'

'Felipe Periera.'

'Mr Periera, before you go off the deep end I have to tell you I have been promised a non-returnable handsome retainer.' She whipped out her mobile phone and scrolled down her details.

'Yes.' She smiled at him. 'Guess what? It hit my bank account today.' She frowned. 'I can't work out the exchange rate in my head but it's a serious sum, wouldn't you agree?'

Felipe's eyebrows rose.

'Have you hacked into my grand-mother's bank account?' he demanded.

'Now that is completely offensive.' Evie snatched back her mobile. 'And unless you withdraw that statement . . . '

She didn't finish her sentence as Felipe responded swiftly.

'I apologise. At times my grand-mother stresses me out.'

'I think she's fantastic,' Evie enthused.

'That is a matter of opinion.'

'Aren't you proud to be the grandson of a Sixties icon?'

'Not when the press pester her — and they do.'

'I'm not a journalist,' Evie insisted.

'Would you like some refreshment?' Felipe indicated the seats on the terrace.

She hesitated.

'I don't want to outstay my welcome.'

For the first time the expression on Felipe's face softened.

'We have other things to argue about, but right now I can see a nice cool jug of freshly squeezed orange juice on the table. I'll get Catherine to fix us some bread and cheese.'

Picking up her suitcase, Evie followed Felipe across the lawn to the paved terrace.

'Make yourself comfortable. I won't be a moment.'

Evie sank into one of the cushioned wickerwork chairs and picked up the abandoned fashion magazine. She flipped through it. Fashion wasn't really her thing but Lesli had insisted she take up this commission.

'You know I can't leave London now and with your knowledge of Portuguese you're the ideal choice.'

'My Portuguese is a bit rusty.'

'Nonsense — it'll soon come back to you,' Lesli said with a dismissive wave of her hand.

Evie had still been reeling from the discovery of learning that the famous Astra Dempsey was married to a member of the family who had ruined her father.

'And don't you have bills to pay? Retainer in advance?' Lesli coaxed.

There had been no arguing with Lesli and a few days later Evie had been on the flight to Portugal. It had been some time since she had visited the country of her birth and with her parents now running specialist breaks for wildlife enthusiasts and living in the Azores, there had been little reason to return to the Algarve.

'Here we are.'

Felipe returned with a tray loaded with bread, cheese and fruit. He poured out two glasses of orange juice and passed one over. He pushed a bowl of fruit towards Evie.

'The apricots and grapes are grown locally, and you have to try some of this honey cake. It is Catherine's speciality.'

He smeared a slice of bread with

some butter then cut himself a generous slice of cheese. Evie followed his example. If it hadn't been for the strangeness of her circumstances Evie would have enjoyed their impromptu picnic on the terrace.

In the distance she could hear the voices of the fishermen in the harbour as they landed the day's catch and mended their nets.

'That was delicious.' Evie sighed. 'You must thank Catherine for me.'

'You can thank her yourself,' Felipe said as Catherine emerged from the house with a tray of coffee and a plate of almond biscuits.

'*Obrigada*, Catherine.' Evie conjured up a smile.

The woman nodded at her but made no comment as she collected up the plates.

'You speak Portuguese?' Felipe asked.

'A bit,' Evie said cautiously, hoping that wouldn't lead to more searching questions.

Felipe nodded then stretched out his long legs and leaned back in his seat.

'Can you tell me exactly what all this is about?' he asked as Catherine went back inside.

Evie took a deep breath.

'I work for a woman called Lesli Scott. She runs an agency.'

'What sort of agency?'

'A modelling agency.'

'You are a model?' Felipe nudged the almond biscuits towards her. 'You have to take one otherwise Catherine will never speak to you again.'

'I'm not sure she's speaking to me now.'

'She'll come round,' Felipe assured her.

'Most of the models I know don't eat almond biscuits for lunch.' Evie took one.

'I work as Lesli's assistant. People get in touch with her if they want someone for an advert or a promotion — or anything really. No two days are the same.'

'I see.'

'Your grandmother contacted Lesli

because she wants someone to make up a catalogue of her fashion collection.'

'For what reason?'

Evie hesitated.

'You really don't know anything about this?'

'Nothing at all. My work takes me all over the world. I visit my grandmother whenever I can. I have rooms here but . . . ' He shrugged. 'Sometimes she does things that are — unwise?'

'She wants to put the collection up for auction.'

'And what does she intend doing with the proceeds?'

'I don't know but I do know she wants to sell the castelo.'

Felipe's almond biscuits fell from his fingers on to the flagstoned terrace. A small brightly coloured bird immediately swooped down to peck up the crumbs.

'Would you mind repeating that?' he asked with a look of incredulity on his face.

'I think you might find yourself

homeless,' Evie added with a smile after she had repeated her story. She was wondering how her father would feel about the irony of history repeating itself.

Secrets of the Attic

It had been a cheap jibe and Evie immediately felt ashamed of her outburst.

'I'm sorry,' she apologised, 'that was rude of me.'

'You have had enough provocation. We haven't exactly been welcoming.' Felipe looked thoughtful as he spoke.

'What do we do now?' Evie asked.

He glanced at his watch.

'Perhaps you had better stay on until I've had a chance to sort things out?'

'I don't want to stay if there's nothing for me to do,' Evie insisted. 'I have an open return ticket so I can fly home any time if my presence is an inconvenience.'

'Could you wait until tomorrow?' Felipe asked. 'I've a busy morning but I promise not to waste your time. I'll ask Catherine to prepare a room for you.'

Evie spent the evening researching

Astra Dempsey. After a solitary supper served by Catherine who barely acknowledged her presence, Evie retired to the room made available to her on the first floor.

Evie could see no expense had been spared. The decorations were cool contemporary and the soft furnishings reflected the Moorish origins of the area.

Bright throws and scatter rugs provided warmth and colour in contrast to the net drapes hanging from the huge windows.

The light was fading and as Evie stood on her small balcony she could see pinpricks of light in the distance as Marina geared up for the evening.

She turned back to her laptop and keyed in Astra's details. There was a wealth of information on her. She epitomised the 60s, with her chiselled cheekbones, green velvet eyes and hint of mystery. She was unique. The camera loved her.

The tiger photo was world famous. It had caused controversy at the time with protestors claiming cruelty saying the animal had been sedated until it was revealed that the tiger was in fact a fake.

The resultant publicity went off the scale. Everyone wanted a part of Astra Dempsey. Then without a word she disappeared off the scene at the height of her career. No reason was ever given for her disappearance.

The rumour mill went into overdrive, one source even suggesting she was dead. There were frequent false sightings of her in the playgrounds of the rich, but none was ever confirmed.

Eventually the rumours died down but every so often she was the subject of exposé type programmes. One persistent journalist had finally tracked her down to Portugal and the old stories were revived but Astra never granted interviews and the reason for her disappearance was still a mystery.

Evie looked at the photos of her and wondered who had taken them. Whoever it was had captured her unique spirit. The name Shaun Merrony emerged from time to time but Evie could find nothing on him, which was strange. Like Astra, he had disappeared off the scene.

Stifling a huge yawn, she stretched her aching limbs and closed down her laptop. She'd contact Lesli tomorrow and update her on all that had happened. Right now all she needed was a shower and a good night's sleep.

★ ★ ★

'Good morning, darling,' Astra greeted her from her seat on the terrace. 'Did you sleep well?'

'I did, thank you.'

'We help ourselves at breakfast.' Astra indicated a buffet table. 'I can recommend the croissants.'

'Can I get you one?'

'I eat very little these days,' Astra admitted, 'and breakfast was never my favourite meal. I'll have another glass of juice, if I may, then come and sit down and tell me your life story. Felipe

23

informs me you speak Portuguese.'

Evie sat down. She should have expected this.

'I was born here,' she admitted.

'Were you really? In Marina?'

'In Faro. My parents moved back to England when I was young.'

'I was born in Newcastle,' Astra admitted, 'and that's something I haven't told anyone for years.'

'Newcastle on Tyne?'

'My publicist put the word round that my mother's father was a lord. It wasn't true but he thought it sounded better — more sophisticated.'

Astra's smile lit up her face. Although she was now in her seventies she was still a beautiful woman.

'The truth was, my lovely father was a miner and my mother worked in a shop.'

'They must have been very proud of all you achieved.'

'Yes and no. My father was old-fashioned. He didn't hold with the London set — in fact he never even visited the capital. I don't remember him going far at all. He had his work, his friends and a small patch of land. He liked to grow vegetables. I inherited his love of flowers. It grieves me that I can't work in my garden so much these days.'

'I've never seen such a beautiful rockery,' Evie said.

'It is lovely, isn't it?' Astra smiled, then continued with her story. 'My mother was the one who encouraged me to follow my dream. She was the real beauty in the family. She had black hair and a beautiful complexion, but in her day young girls were at the beck and call of their families and there was little opportunity for her to better herself.

'She loved my father and they were very happy together but sometimes I'd catch a wistful look in her eye when I told her of some of the things I'd done.'

Evie shifted uncomfortably in her chair. She wasn't sure Felipe would approve of his grandmother telling Evie about her past but before she could say anything Astra began speaking again.

'One day we went swimming in the local baths. I think it was the only chance my mother got to show off her figure. She looked stunning in her costume. A man approached us and asked if we'd ever thought of a career in modelling.

'Of course, neither of us had. My mother turned down his offer but she wasn't going to stand in my way. To cut a long story short a month later I found myself in London.'

'How old were you?'

'Seventeen, still a minor, but I was one of the lucky ones. The agent who approached us was thoroughly respectable. He provided a female chaperone, a lovely lady. She introduced herself to my parents and assured them she would take every care of me — and she did.

'I was only allowed to date carefully vetted men. That was my selling point, I suppose you could say — my unavailability. The scene was buzzing but I had little idea of all that was going on around me. All I wanted to do was wear lovely dresses and model. I suppose that makes me sound empty?'

'Not at all,' Evie insisted. 'You had a successful career.'

'I used to send money home for my parents but you know what? When I went back I discovered my mother had banked the lot for me. She couldn't understand I wanted her to spend it on herself.' She smiled. 'I could do nothing to change her mind, so when she passed on I made sure it all went to a local charity.' Astra nodded towards Evie's untouched croissant. 'Eat your breakfast.'

'Are you sure you don't want anything?'

'I don't sleep well,' Astra admitted, 'so I hope you won't think me rude if I have a little snooze?'

As Evie ate, Catherine hovered in the background. She pretended to be dusting but all the while Evie could feel her eyes watching her every move.

'This is for you.'

The sound of Astra's voice made Evie jump. She slipped a small pouch across the table.

'What is it?' Evie asked.

'The key to the attic.' Astra put a finger to her lips. 'Our secret.'

'I don't understand.' Evie frowned.

'No-one goes up there these days. It's been locked up for ages but you can take a look.'

'I'm not sure I should.'

'Seize the day.' Astra gave a saucy wink. 'Look out, Catherine's coming.'

She closed her eyes and pretended to be asleep. Evie slid the pouch into her pocket and smiling at Catherine, but receiving no acknowledgement in return, she made her way back indoors.

Evie was under no illusions. For her age Astra was as smart as they come. She knew how to use her looks to get what she wanted and Evie suspected she wasn't above using emotional blackmail to have her own way.

She had pretended not to remember

why Evie was there, but if that was so why had she given her the key to the attic?

Evie paused at the foot of the stairs. Felipe said he had a busy morning. Catherine was fussing over Astra on the terrace. There was nothing to stop Evie investigating.

Evie tiptoed up to the top floor and turned the key in the lock. The door's hinges protested from lack of oil but eventually creaked open. Glancing over her shoulder Evie slipped inside and let out a sigh of relief before biting down a gasp of surprise.

She didn't know what she had been expecting — but not this. The attic was fitted out like a backstage fashion house dressing room. In one corner stood a huge floor-to-ceiling mirror and in another a French-style dressing table, displaying more mirrors that could be angled to catch the light.

A chair in one corner bore evidence of neglect. The upholstery had faded from too much exposure to the sun and the cushions were frayed, the paintwork chipped. Long-dead flies dangled from ancient cobwebs.

Evie looked along the wall to where a gallery of photos covered every surface. She took a tentative step forward, her mouth dropping open as she recognised some of the famous faces of the day.

Underneath a patterned throw Evie discovered a trunk hidden away behind a dressmaker's dummy. Falling to her knees she managed to ease open the lid. She sat back on her heels. The overload on her senses was too much. The trunk was full of dresses, all in good condition and professionally stored. Evie unearthed a black and white plaid mini coat. She couldn't resist trying it on. It fitted her like a glove. She twirled in front of a mirror.

Hearing voices in the garden outside, she hastily refolded the coat and closed the chest. Glancing towards the door her eyes fell on a small built-in wardrobe under the eaves. Careful not to bang her head Evie pushed the door. It slid back. Stepping forward she peered inside and stifled a shriek of shock.

The shape confronting her wasn't human — it was a scarlet dress on a hanger, perhaps the most famous dress in the world. She looking at the Tiger Dress. It was draped in a see-through cover but there was no mistaking it. Pinned to the cover was a copy of the famous photo.

Careful not to lose her balance, Evie stepped backwards out of the cupboard.

'Exactly what do you think you are doing here?' a voice behind her demanded.

A Matter of Trust

'You have no right to be here. Where did you get this?'

Still trying to get her senses under control Evie could only blink at Felipe as he snatched the key out of the door. Without waiting for her answer, he stood square in front of her.

'I suggest you leave — now.'

On trembling legs, Evie began her descent of the stairs. Behind her she could hear Felipe locking the door. Catherine was waiting for them at the foot of the stairs.

Evie realised it had been Catherine's voice she had heard through the open skylight probably telling Felipe that the unwanted guest was up to no good.

Ignoring her, Evie descended another flight of stairs and bumped into a sleepy Astra wandering along the second floor landing.

'There you are.' She smiled. 'Shall we have some tea?' She caught sight of the hovering Catherine who seemed reluctant to let Evie out of her sight. She hurried away to do her mistress's bidding.

'Do you know you've got cobwebs in your hair?' Astra picked a dead spider out of Evie's fringe. 'What have you been doing?'

'I caught her poking around the attic.' Felipe came up behind Evie. 'Did you give Ms Quinta your key?'

Astra blinked at him sleepily.

'Attic?' she mumbled. 'Key?'

'Never mind,' Felipe soothed his grandmother. 'Have you taken your tonic?' he enquired in a softer tone.

'You know if you didn't frown quite so much you might almost be handsome, darling.' Astra patted his face. 'Don't you think so, Evie?'

Evie was saved from replying by Felipe urging his grandmother to sit down.

'I do feel a bit woozy,' she admitted. 'Let's go on to the terrace.'

Felipe guided Astra down the remaining stairs and settled her down in her canopied swinger.

Catherine nudged Evie out of the way with a tray of tea things while Felipe fussed over Astra. With her habitual glare at Evie, Catherine began talking to Felipe in rapid Portuguese. Although she had her back to her Evie caught several words.

Biting down the urge to yell at Catherine that she was not a spy or a thief Evie waited patiently until Catherine finished speaking, wondering what would be Felipe's next move.

He sat down opposite Evie and bit absently into one of Catherine's biscuits. Determined not to be the first to speak, Evie waited for Felipe to start the dialogue.

'I've been into the village.' He spoke carefully, subjecting her to a searching look. 'And my notary tells me it would be wise to draw up a contract.'

'What sort of contract?'

'We could call it a term of reference if you like.'

'I'm not signing anything,' Evie said firmly, 'and just for the record I resent being accused of poking around in the attic. I was there with Astra's permission. I didn't break in, neither am I a spy nor have I any intention of stealing anything.'

'You understood what Catherine was saying?' Felipe raised an enquiring eyebrow.

'Enough to know she wasn't singing my praises.'

'She's very protective of my grandmother as I've already explained.'

'That doesn't give her the right to say things about me that aren't true so I suggest you go back to your legal eagle and tell him no deal.'

Evie wished Felipe wouldn't smile at her. It was much easier to make a forceful point when he was on the attack.

'Have I said something to amuse you?' Evie demanded.

'I like your style,' he admitted, 'but there really is no need to go over the top.'

'I was merely standing up for myself,' Evie backtracked.

'I approve,' Felipe said with old-fashioned courtesy.

'Look, I think the best thing is for us to forget all about this catalogue idea. Astra doesn't remember suggesting it. You don't trust me. Catherine thinks I am a female spy. Why don't I draw a line under the whole incident and catch the next flight home?'

'You've been paid in advance,' Felipe pointed out.

Evie grimaced. He had a point. Lesli would not be best pleased if she walked out on a job.

'What sort of contract did you have in mind?' she asked.

'Something along the lines of you stating your position here and what exactly you intend to do. The notary can witness your statement.'

'I don't know what I intend to do,' Evie pointed out.

'What were you told?' Felipe asked.

'Astra wanted to make up a catalogue

of her fashion collection because she was considering putting it up for auction.'

'And the bit about the castelo being sold off?'

Evie wriggled uncomfortably in her seat.

'I may have exaggerated that bit,' she admitted.

'Good — because I've double checked with the notary. Astra only has a lifetime interest in the castelo. She cannot sell it. It is entailed.'

'To whom?'

'The next Vicente male heir.'

'That would be you, wouldn't it?'

'I am a Periera. My mother Cassandra was Astra's daughter.'

'I see.'

'Eduardo Vicente is my uncle. His father was my grandfather's brother. He hopes to inherit one day.'

'Hopes?'

'There is some legal disagreement over the exact details, but that is nothing you need to concern yourself with now. What we need to discuss is Astra's collection. We should have it valued and the best way to start would be to catalogue it. Will you do the job?'

'How long will it take?'

'I'm not sure until we start going through everything.'

'And you want me to sign a contract before I can start.'

'Would you?' Felipe looked earnest. 'It's for your benefit as well as the family's. We can hammer out the details with the clerk this afternoon. He's promised to have it ready for signature by tomorrow after which we can make a start.'

'You'd be here to help me?'

'Not all the time,' Felipe admitted, 'but I'll be on hand whenever I can.'

'I need to update Lesli,' Evie insisted.

'As you wish.' Felipe glanced at his watch. 'I have one or two things I need to attend to but I'll be back by three o'clock. I hope you will still be here.' He stood up. Again his smile totally transformed his face.

'I think we'd best leave Astra here, don't you?' He gestured to his grandmother who had fallen asleep, her cup of tea untouched.

'Do you want me to keep an eye on her?'

'Catherine will do that. You go and make your call.'

'Hi, there.' Lesli appeared on the laptop screen. 'What gives? I was beginning to think you'd eloped with Felipe Periera.'

'You know Astra's grandson?'

'Not personally, but I know of him. I have to admit that until I started my research I didn't realise who he was.'

'So who is he?' Evie asked, completely baffled.

'You haven't heard of him?'

'No.'

'He does wonderful wildlife photographs of endangered wild animals. It helps raise their profile and people's awareness of their plight. Check him out. He's won awards and there is a stack of stuff about him on the net.

What's with the puzzled look?' Lesli asked.

'Nothing adds up here, Lesli.'

'Talk me through it.'

'No-one knew anything about me. There's a sort of housekeeper here who seems to have me down as an industrial spy. Astra's flaky to say the least,' Evie paused. 'Felipe's accused me of being a hacker and I want to come home.'

'Don't be such a wimp,' Lesli snorted. 'Sign his contract and get on with the job. That's what you're being paid for. Now was there anything else?'

Evie shook her head. Talking to Lesli had done nothing to allay her fears. She didn't know of Evie's family history with the Vicente family and Evie had been reluctant to bring it up in case Catherine was hovering and overheard.

Evie had only ever heard her speak Portuguese but that didn't mean to say she couldn't understand some English.

'Right, well, I'm sure you're busy. Keep in touch.'

'Your lunch is ready.' Catherine's

appearance in the doorway made Evie jump. She realised she had been right not to divulge too much of her past to Lesli while she was hovering outside her door.

Evie followed her down to the terrace. Catherine indicated the plate of sardines and salad and another bowl of fresh fruit.

As Evie enjoyed her light lunch she wondered if Felipe had insisted Catherine made sure she didn't go hungry. She remembered charcoal-grilled sardines being a traditional dish of the area and she had to admit Catherine was a good cook. She bit into a fleshy apricot, savouring its velvet sweetness.

Felipe appeared around the far corner of the terrace as she was wiping the juice from her chin.

'We're all set,' he informed her. 'Our appointment is for three o'clock.'

The notary's office was on the second floor of an elegant neo-classical building.

'I can smell floor polish and lemons,'

Evie said as they mounted the stairs.

'Carlos Diego insists on the highest standards from his cleaners. He says it creates a good impression.'

'Does he own the building?' Evie asked in surprise.

'The family does,' Felipe replied. 'They have lived in Marina for years. Carlos occupies the top floor so he doesn't have far to travel to work every day.' He held open the door for Evie. 'But today he is not here. His senior clerk will draft the contract then tomorrow Carlos will call by the castelo and we can do the official signing.'

The drafting of the contract was a leisurely business, interrupted by refreshment breaks and frequent revisions of clauses that did not meet Felipe's exacting standards. Evie realised she had underestimated his business acumen.

He was well aware of the cultural value of Astra's personal effects. With their impeccable provenance he felt it would be wise to insert a clause in Evie's contract that she was not to be held responsible should anything go astray.

'I fear my grandmother can be a little forgetful,' he explained, when Evie was about to protest. 'It really is for your protection. She is quite likely to pick something up, look at it, put it down somewhere then completely forget all about it.'

With the clerk promising to have the document drawn up in time for their next day's appointment, Felipe suggested Evie join him for a drink.

'You're in no hurry to get back to the castelo, are you?' he asked when Evie hesitated.

'No, but what about Astra?'

'Catherine will stay on.'

'Surely her own family will need her.'

'She is a widow and her daughter is in Faro. Now, I can recommend the rosé.'

★　★　★

It was late by the time they returned to the castelo. Catherine was seated in

Astra's sun lounger nursing a cup of coffee.

'I'm sorry if we kept you,' Felipe apologised.

Catherine subjected Evie to one of her looks before dismissing Felipe's apology with something that resembled a smile.

'It does not matter. Your grand-mother did not want to go to bed early so we stayed on the terrace, talking. You have eaten?'

'Thank you, yes. Would you like me to escort you home?' Felipe asked.

'That won't be necessary. How was Carlos?'

'We didn't see him.'

'That's a pity. It would have been a good opportunity to introduce him to Ms Quinta.'

'He will be here tomorrow.'

'Did you explain that his family has handled the legal affairs of your family for many years?'

Evie felt a shiver of apprehension creep up her spine. Was Catherine hinting at something? Had her father had dealings with Carlos's family?

'I wish you good night,' Catherine said, leaving them alone on the terrace.

'She will get used to you in time,' Felipe said, 'but until then I would ask you to be patient. She distrusts strangers. We've had reporters trying to gain access to my grandmother. They want to write her life story. She has always refused to speak to them but they don't give up.'

Evie yawned behind the back of her hand.

'Go to bed,' Felipe insisted, 'and thank you for a lovely evening.'

He bent forward and kissed her on the cheek. Taken by surprise, Evie stumbled through the patio doors and went upstairs to her room. For all his fine words she did not trust Felipe Periera. She wasn't sure he trusted her, yet illogically she found his company stimulating.

With the sound of the crickets chirruping in the garden she fell into a dreamless sleep.

Chance Meeting

Evie awoke refreshed and ready to face the day. She pulled back the shutters. Early morning sunshine streamed in. After a quick shower she decided to go for a jog. It had been a week since she had had any proper exercise.

Letting herself out through a side door she followed a small path down to the harbour. The fishermen on the quayside called out a greeting as she jogged past. Waving cheerfully, she decided to follow the natural curve of the coastline.

The morning air was stimulating and Evie's feet pounded the sandy path, building up a steady rhythm.

'*Bom dia, senhorita,*' a voice greeted her.

Evie was breathing too hard to do any more than gasp a reply.

'I am sorry,' the man continued in

English, 'I did not mean to startle you.' Like Evie he was dressed in shorts and trainers. 'May I join you?'

'How did you know I was English?' Evie asked.

'Word gets round,' he explained with a charming smile. He was good-looking although slightly overweight and there was a suggestion of grey in his sleek dark hair.

Evie returned his friendly smile.

'Shall we continue on round the harbour?' he suggested. 'It's a lovely run and I often take advantage of the early morning sunshine. It gets too hot later in the day to do anything but sit at my desk for hours on end. I feel I should get some exercise.'

'I feel the same,' Evie replied.

'Are you a friend of the Vicente family?' he asked.

Evie bit her lip, unsure how to answer. For all she knew, her companion could be an undercover journalist intent on finding out all that was going on at the castelo.

'Sorry, I'm not very good at talking and running at the same time.' She waved a regretful hand.

'I understand.'

Eventually she sensed her jogging partner was flagging and with her lungs bursting and her singlet sticking to her back Evie was also forced to slow down.

'Thank goodness.' The man doubled over. 'You set a mean pace. I think I'm going to have to throw in the towel. Perhaps we can do it again some time. See you later.'

With a cheery wave he turned and jogged slowly back the way they had come. Evie frowned. What had he meant by that last remark? When would he see her again?

Surely he wasn't a stalker? Yet he knew she was English and that she was staying at the castelo. With a thoughtful frown she headed back the way she had come.

After another refreshing shower she made her way down to the terrace. Felipe was waiting for her.

'You have been out?' he asked.

'I went for a jog. That is allowed?'

'Of course. I would have liked to join you but I am pressed for time.'

Evie decided not to tell Felipe about her companion. He was sure to criticise her for talking to a stranger.

'I had a telephone call this morning from the notary. The contract will be ready to sign early this afternoon. After that you will be free to come and go as you please. Meanwhile the attic door will stay locked.'

'You take your security seriously,' Evie couldn't help teasing him. 'You haven't got an unbalanced first wife locked away somewhere have you?'

Felipe frowned.

'It is no joking matter. For the moment you are forbidden to go up there.'

Evie glanced at the hovering Catherine. Again she had the suspicion the woman understood every word that was being said. She changed the subject.

'Where is Astra this morning?'

'She will be down shortly. Catherine has just taken up her breakfast.'

'Is there anything I can do in the meantime?'

'Avó mentioned something about a scrapbook. You and my grandmother could look through that together.'

Evie lingered over her coffee after Felipe had driven off. She was still having serious doubts about the wisdom of accepting this assignment. Nothing was as it seemed and she couldn't help feeling there were bigger issues at stake than merely cataloguing a collection of dresses.

'There you are.' Looking supremely elegant in a pink shirtwaist dress and wearing a fetching sun hat and designer dark glasses, Astra strolled on to the terrace, clutching a large album. 'Come and sit beside me.'

The swinger rocked slowly backwards and forwards as Astra leafed through her scrapbook, a smile of pleasure on her face.

'They were good times,' she said to Evie, 'vibrant and exciting. I loved the life. I met so many people you would not believe — important, influential people, but like everyone else on the scene I didn't realise it at the time. It was just a way of life going from party to party, receptions, photo shoots, flying in private aircraft . . . '

Evie peered over her shoulder. There were numerous publicity photos, many with the obligatory angry young men posing astride motorcycles or sitting at the wheel of powerful sports cars.

Astra's presence added symbolism to the pictures. She held herself aloof, apart from the scene as if she were looking on from another dimension. Whoever took the photos knew exactly what they were doing and how to get the best out of her.

Astra pointed to a photo of a man scowling at the camera. He didn't look part of the scene. His moody expression indicated he would rather be anywhere else than in the middle of yet another party. Evie had seen a similar expression on Felipe's face when she had first been introduced to him.

The eyes reflected world-weariness unusual in one so young. Here was a man who would always be searching for something.

'Who is he?' Evie asked, intrigued.

Astra paused for so long Evie thought she wasn't going to answer.

'His name was Shaun Merrony,' she said. Her voice sounded raw as if speaking his name gave her grief.

'Who was he?'

'A photographer. He didn't like being on the other side of the lens,' Astra confided. 'When I took this photo he was mad as a box of frogs. He tried to get me to destroy the shot but I ran away from him and he couldn't catch me.'

'Were you close?'

'Very.' Astra spoke in such a low voice Evie wasn't sure she had actually replied. She snapped the album shut and Evie sensed further questions would be an invasion of privacy.

'Your driver will be here shortly,

senhora,' Catherine interrupted them. 'You haven't forgotten your hair appointment?'

'I don't want to go,' Astra insisted. 'I want to stay and talk to Evie.'

Catherine snorted. Eyeing the scrapbook that Evie had picked up during the exchange, Catherine snatched it out of her hands.

'Senhor Periera asks that everything is kept away from prying eyes.'

'Evie wasn't prying,' Astra said. 'We were looking at my past.'

'Come along.' Still keeping a firm hold of the scrapbook, Catherine ushered Astra indoors.

Alone on the terrace Evie typed Felipe's name into her mobile phone to see what she could find out about him. There was a wealth of information detailing his extensive career.

Intrigued, Evie read how he shunned the limelight and was rarely photographed but he used his professional skills to highlight the plight of endangered wildlife species, something he was passionate about.

He bullied governments and chivvied ministers into sitting up and taking notice of what he had to say about the environment. It was rumoured he had been responsible for several changes of ministerial policies. His rate of success had been phenomenal.

So why hadn't Evie heard of him? She scrolled down pages of text. Apart from one grainy picture there were no photographs of Felipe. Neither was there any mention of him being Astra Dempsey's grandson. It was as if the pair of them hated all forms of personal publicity, yet it had been their life.

Was Felipe's aversion to publicity a spin-off of Astra's unexplained disappearance off the scene? Had something happened to her and had that something rubbed off on Felipe? If so, it was no wonder he didn't want Evie poking around in the attic.

An auction of Astra's dresses would revive all the old stories and new theories as to what had happened would probably be invented. Fake news was the name of the game these days and media coverage was far more sophisticated than in the 60s. It wasn't so easy to do a disappearing act.

Evie stood up and stretched her legs. Astra must have worked hard to create the English country garden effect. There was evidence everywhere of her love of flowers, from the rockery to the sweet smelling rose bushes and the pungent organic herbs. She inhaled the mixture of fragrances, totally understanding Astra's reluctance to leave her beautiful Castle of Flowers.

The sound of car wheels drew Evie back to the present. Moments later, Felipe emerged on the terrace, accompanied by a man she instantly recognised.

'Evie,' he called over. 'Let me introduce you to my notary — Carlos Diego.'

'We've already met.' Carlos came forward and extended his hand.

'You have — when?' Felipe didn't look too pleased by this piece of information.

'This morning. We went jogging together. Have you recovered? My legs are still aching.'

Evie shook Carlos's hand, noting he was the first person since she had arrived at the castelo to offer her a genuine friendly welcome.

False Accusations

'Thank you, Evie,' Carlos recapped his pen.

'That all seems to be in order. Was there anything else?' He looked at Felipe.

'Not today, thank you.'

The two men shook hands.

'I'll see you out,' Felipe said.

'There's no need. After all this time I should know the way.' He smiled at Evie. 'My father handled the legal affairs of the Vicente family for many years,' he explained, 'and when he retired I took over the reins.'

Evie ignored the feeling of apprehension creeping up her spine. Would Carlos make the connection between her father, Francisco, and the Vicente family? She hoped not.

Felipe's mobile phone burst into life. 'Excuse me, I have to take this call.'

'I'm glad we've got a chance to have a private word,' Carlos confided after Felipe had left the room.

'Yes?' The lump of nervousness in Evie's throat made it difficult to speak.

'I hope you don't mind my asking . . .' Carlos began.

'Go on,' Evie urged. If the worst was to come then it would be better to get it over with sooner rather than later.

'I wondered if you would like to come out with me for dinner one evening?'

This was not what Evie had been expecting and for a moment she could only stare open mouthed at Carlos.

'You don't like the idea?'

'Of course, yes, no . . . I mean you took me by surprise, that's all. I'd love to have dinner with you.'

As she spoke Felipe came back into the room. From his expression it was obvious he had overheard her acceptance of Carlos's invitation.

'Good,' Carlos said, unaware of the increased tension in the room. 'I'll give you a call and we can arrange something. Felipe.' He nodded and, picking up his briefcase, left the room.

'I presume I am allowed evenings off,' Evie said in justification before Felipe could speak.

'Just see your social life doesn't interfere with your work.'

'What work?' Evie was quick to interject. 'So far all I've done is look through a trunk of dresses. Astra's scrapbook was snatched away from me the moment I was bold enough to glance inside it and I've been banned from going back up into the attic.'

'All that is about to change,' Felipe replied. 'From tomorrow you can go where you like. I have been called away and I have to leave immediately. I'll give Catherine the key.'

'Won't you even trust me with a key?' Evie demanded.

'It would be unfortunate,' Felipe chose his words carefully, 'should it go astray.'

'Catherine is just as capable of losing a key as I would be.'

'Agreed, but she has been with us a long time.'

Evie could feel her lip curling in disbelief.

'What do I have to do to convince you I am not about to make off with the contents of Astra's attic tucked away in my suitcase?'

'I do trust you,' Felipe insisted.

'Have a good trip. I'll see you when you get back, if I'm still here.'

Evie made to turn her back on him.

'I hope you're not thinking of walking out on us. You've signed a contract, remember?' Felipe made a movement towards her, his fingers touching her elbow.

'I've never walked out on a job yet.' Evie wished she could wriggle out of his grasp. 'But there's always a first time. You see, I've never been accused of being a thief before.'

'I'll leave you to your duties,' he said and turned to go. His footsteps echoed down the stone corridor as Evie watched him stride away from her, then she decided she had to update Lesli on the latest developments.

'Does the name Shaun Merrony mean anything to you?' she asked after Lesli had finished delivering her views on clients who treated her assistant like a criminal.

'It rings a vague bell,' Lesli admitted. 'Why?'

'Do you think you could find out who he was?'

'Leave it with me,' Lesli promised. 'Glad you're seeing this thing through,' she added. 'The Sixties are hot right now. If Astra does get this auction under way media interest will be epic.'

'I'm not sure that's what she wants.'

'She may not be able to avoid it.'

★ ★ ★

The next morning Evie stood in front of the door to the attic and turned the handle. It didn't budge. Stifling her exasperation she went in search of Catherine.

'May I have the key to the attic?' she asked in English. When Catherine looked blankly at her, Evie repeated her request in Portuguese.

'No.' Catherine shook her head, a guilty look flashing across her face as she realised Evie spoke Portuguese.

'Why not?' Evie demanded.

'You must not go up there alone and I am busy.'

'This is ridiculous.' Evie was now growing seriously annoyed.

Catherine shrugged and turned away. Controlling her anger, Evie went in search of Astra. She found her on the terrace.

'Darling, whatever's wrong?'

'Catherine has the key to the attic but she won't give it to me.'

'Why ever not?'

'She says she's too busy to accompany me up there. I don't need a chaperone, Astra, but I do need to get on. If I am banned from doing my job on the whim of a housekeeper, then I have to tell you I'm going home.'

'Darling, of course you must have the key. I'll tell you what we'll do. I'll give you my duplicate then I can pretend to have a funny turn and distract Catherine to give you a chance to get upstairs without being noticed.'

'I'm not sure we can do that.' Evie hesitated, remembering how angry Felipe was the last time she had borrowed Astra's key.

'It's my house,' Astra said in an unexpectedly firm tone of voice, 'and what I say goes. Now get me my bag. It's over there.'

★   ★   ★

Evie pushed the attic door open, then, pocketing the key, she edged into the room. Armed with a notebook and her mobile in order to take photos she looked round, wondering where to start.

How long it would take her to catalogue Evie's collection she didn't know but Lesli expected her to be back in the office in two weeks' time.

Evie decided to attack the trunk first. It contained not only Astra's dresses but all the accessories. There were bags, shoes, scarves, hats and some costume jewellery. Evie decided to concentrate on the dresses.

Absorbed in her task of listing every item and cross-referencing it with a photo she lost track of time.

Pausing every so often to admire the creations so indicative of the 60s, she decided her personal favourite was a purple mini dress. Evie could imagine wearing it with knee-high white boots and perhaps the black and white coat she had discovered on her first visit to the attic.

Evie eventually decided she had done enough for one day. She needed to transcribe her notes and sort her photos into some sort of order.

Carefully replacing the listed items back into the trunk she took one last look round before closing the door. She was about to lock the door before an outraged Catherine verbally attacked her.

'You have deceived me.' She pushed Evie to one side and snatched the key out of her grasp. 'Where did you get this?'

Restraining the urge to snatch it back, Evie maintained her calm.

'Astra gave it to me and I'd like it back, please. I need to lock the door.'

'You are never to go up there again.'

'I think you're overstepping your authority.'

'I have all the authority I need.'

'So do I and my authority is in writing, signed and witnessed by the notary.'

'Stop raising your voice. You're upsetting my mistress. She has been unwell and I have been attending to her. I suppose that was when you stole her key.'

'I have stolen nothing.'

At that moment a shadow appeared at the far end of the landing. Evie's heart sank. She knew exactly who it was.

Sinister Threats

'There is no need to bother yourself further with this, Catherine,' Felipe spoke in a firm voice.

'As you wish.' Conceding she had lost the argument, Catherine made her way downstairs.

'Aren't you going to do anything about Catherine?' Evie demanded.

'I just did.'

'Her behaviour is outrageous.'

'We have to make allowances.'

'I've done nothing but make allowances.'

'I'd noticed.'

Evie ignored the teasing note in Felipe's voice.

'When you're here butter wouldn't melt in her mouth but the moment I'm alone with her she's a completely different person.'

'Then it's as well I don't plan on going away any time soon, isn't it?'

'Do you really charm politicians around to your way of thinking?' Evie demanded.

'I beg your pardon?'

'You need diplomatic skills to save baby hippos or the great white something or other, don't you?'

'You've lost me, I'm afraid.'

'How about taking me up as one of your lost causes? I could really do with some help.'

Felipe's calm manner made Evie realise that no matter what she said he would never take her side against Catherine.

'It doesn't matter.' She shook her head, regretting her impulsive words.

'Then let us change the subject.' Felipe appeared unruffled by her outburst. 'How has your day gone?'

'I didn't realise the enormity of the task,' Evie admitted.

'I could help.'

'What did you have in mind?'

'Why don't I do the photography for you if you do the writing up?' he suggested. 'Shall we start in the morning?'

Evie spent the evening writing up more notes. Felipe had apologised for not being able to join her for supper.

'I have yet another meeting to attend,' he said with an unenthusiastic look on his face. 'I'll probably be back late. It takes time to put the wheels in motion to save baby hippos,' he added, his lips twisting into an impish smile that brought a flush to Evie's face.

She lowered her eyes and mumbled an apology for her earlier rudeness.

'I'll catch up with you tomorrow,' Felipe said.

Moments later she heard his car drive off in the direction of Marina.

*   *   *

The next morning, with the help of a part-time gardener, she and Felipe manhandled the trunk down from the attic and out on to the terrace. Astra was as excited as a child as she watched

Evie lay out several of the dresses ready for Felipe to photograph them.

'This was one of my favourites.' She pounced on the purple mini dress and held it up against Evie. 'You must try it on.'

'No,' Evie protested, 'I couldn't.'

'Nonsense, you have a lovely figure. It could have been made for you.'

'My grandmother is right,' Felipe intervened, 'you should model the dress. It would make a better photograph.'

'I am not a model and the dress is far too short for me.'

'All the better to show off your legs,' Astra insisted.

Realising this was another argument she was not going to win, Evie went indoors to change into the dress. Astra was swinging to and fro on her hammock when Evie returned to the terrace.

'I was right,' she crowed. 'Felipe, you have to agree with me. Doesn't Evie look beautiful?'

'Indeed she does,' he agreed, raising an eyebrow.

'You know the first time I wore that dress I received three proposals of marriage. Can you believe it?'

'And did you accept them?' Felipe asked.

'It wouldn't have been proper to accept more than one.'

'Of course — but when did you ever do what was considered proper?' Filipe teased his grandmother.

Evie was beginning to suspect his brusque manner was a cover for a more caring personality. Astra positively glowed from all the attention her grandson was giving her.

'Now why don't you have a snooze? Evie and I have work to do and we don't want you tiring yourself out.'

'I am feeling a little sleepy,' Astra admitted as he led her back to her sun lounger. 'You will wake me in time for tea, won't you?'

'What is it about you English and your tea?' Felipe asked as he finished photographing Evie.

'With an English grandmother you don't need me to answer that question,' Evie said, realising as she spoke that she knew very little about Felipe's background.

She knew his mother, Cassandra, was Astra's daughter but there had been no mention of his father or why Astra and Mauricio had brought him up. There were no family photographs dotted about the castelo, even though Astra had kept many pictures from her modelling days.

'I thought I heard voices.'

A man strolled down the footpath leading into the garden from the front of the castelo. He looked every inch the European aristocrat in designer polo shirt, tailored chinos and tasselled loafers, although his complexion bore evidence of too much good living.

'And who is this?' he asked, eyeing the mini dress Evie was wearing. His intense look made her feel uncomfortable. 'Isn't that dress length a little indecent?'

Evie felt the happy atmosphere on the terrace dissolve in an instant.

'I'd better go and change,' she excused herself and went back inside.

'Senhor Eduardo is here?' Catherine was as usual hovering in the drawing-room.

'Who is he?' Evie asked.

'Senhor Felipe's uncle. He is the son of Senhor Mauricio's younger brother.'

'I see.'

Evie wriggled back into her leggings and top.

'He lives in the village but he would like to live in the castelo.'

'Why doesn't he? There's plenty of room.'

'Because he does not have the right. I will make the tea.'

Evie hesitated, wondering what she should do. If Eduardo wanted to discuss family matters with Felipe, it might be better if she made herself scarce but the sound of approaching footsteps caused her to hesitate.

'There you are.' Felipe looked relieved to find her still standing in the drawing-room.

'Catherine's making some tea,' Evie explained.

'Then come and join us on the terrace — please,' Felipe added.

Eduardo was seated in one of the padded loungers, his narrowed eyes surveying the view.

'Eduardo, this is Evie Quinta,' Felipe introduced her. 'She is helping Astra to catalogue her fashion collection.'

Eduardo did not bother to stand up and barely glanced in Evie's direction.

'I had heard some gossip that your grandmother wants to raise money. Don't you think I should have been personally informed of her financial problems rather than hear the news second hand?'

'Without wishing to sound rude, Eduardo, Astra's affairs are none of your business.'

'I disagree. It is very much my business if she intends selling the castelo.' He sat up angrily. 'She cannot do that and you cannot inherit, either. It is entailed through the male line and

73

I am the next male heir.'

Although Eduardo spoke in rapid Portuguese Evie had no difficulty keeping up with him. She felt sorry for Felipe. This was not a conversation that should be conducted in front of herself, or Astra, even though she had fallen asleep.

'I won't stay for tea.' Eduardo struggled to his feet. 'I merely came to check on the situation and I see my worst fears are confirmed.' He glanced at the clothes strewn over the terrace with a look of disgust. 'You haven't heard the last of this,' he threatened as he left.

'I must apologise for my uncle's manners,' Felipe said to Evie.

'Was that Eduardo?' Astra enquired, stifling a yawn.

'Nothing for you to bother about,' Felipe soothed her concern.

'Has he been causing more trouble?' Catherine bustled on to the terrace and Felipe relieved her of the tea tray. 'Your grandmother is upset,' she said, and although she spoke to Felipe, Evie had the feeling the rebuke was directed at her.

'Come along,' she addressed Astra. 'You have had enough sun for one day. You can drink your tea upstairs.'

Like a docile child Astra allowed Catherine to lead her indoors.

'I'm sorry you had to witness that distressing scene,' Felipe said. 'I presume you understood what was being said?'

Evie nodded.

Felipe took a deep breath.

'When my grandfather died seven years ago Eduardo tried to have Astra evicted from the castelo.'

'That's dreadful,' Evie said, appalled by the idea of such treatment.

'Agreed,' Felipe said. 'She has a lifetime interest in the castelo and Eduardo knows that. What we are not so sure of is what will happen when,' Felipe paused, 'nature takes its course.'

'Perhaps you should discuss the situation with Carlos?' Evie suggested.

'He's fully aware of Eduardo's claim. I do not know where I stand and to be frank I do not mind. I have no emotional attachment to the castelo, but what does annoy me is that Eduardo has no interest in it, either. He accuses Astra of wanting to sell the property but that is exactly what he would do should he inherit.'

'Can he do that?'

'I'm not sure. He will try — of that I am sure.'

'I see.' Evie lapsed into silence.

'Eduardo is exactly like his father. Over the years their extravagant lifestyle almost bankrupted the estate. All the properties and business interests were sold off to meet their debts until the castelo was the only remaining asset in the property portfolio.'

'The vineyards?' Evie asked carefully, hoping Felipe wouldn't ask how she knew about them.

'They had to go too,' Felipe admitted. 'My great-grandfather was still alive at the time and there was nothing my grandfather could do about it. Several families were evicted. It was not a good time for the family. By the time Mauricio inherited there was nothing left so even if he had wanted to he couldn't pay anyone back. It was something that weighed heavily on his conscience.'

'I'm sorry,' Evie said. If what Felipe had told her was true then it did explain a lot of what happened to her father.

'My grandparents did not have an easy life. I think that's why Astra took to her garden. It was therapy away from all their problems.'

'You don't have to tell me any more,' Evie insisted.

Felipe looked at her in surprise as if he had only just remembered to whom he was talking.

'You're right. You are not here to listen to my troubles but a word of advice ... Should Eduardo come calling again, I suggest you have as little to do with him as possible.'

'Is he the reason the attic is locked?' Evie wasn't sure why she had asked the question.

'He has been guilty of poking about the place,' Felipe acknowledged, 'although what he is expecting to find I can't imagine.'

'I'll bear your advice in mind,' Evie said.

A reluctant smile crossed Felipe's face.

'Families are something we all have to live with, through good times and bad.'

Evie looked at the tray Catherine had left on the table.

'At the risk of sounding English,' she smiled back at Felipe, 'would you like some tea?'

Unhappy Story

'There is a call for you.' Catherine was in the hall standing by the telephone.

'*Obrigada.*' Evie lapsed into Portuguese as she took the receiver from her.

'Evie? Carlos Diego.'

'Hello. What can I do for you?'

'About our date? I wondered if you would like to go to the music festa tonight?'

'The festa? I'm not sure,' Evie hesitated.

'You should go,' Catherine interrupted, making Evie jump. She hadn't been aware she was still standing by her side.

'Who's that?' Carlos asked.

'Catherine.'

'Then take her advice and come with me. You'll enjoy yourself. There's going to be a special open-air performance of the ballet 'Sleeping Beauty'. I've got tickets. We could have supper after-wards.'

'Who is on the telephone?' Felipe came into the hall.

'Senhor Diego. He wishes to take Senhorita Evie to the ballet tonight. You would not mind, would you?'

'Catherine.' Evie was growing irritated by her interruptions. 'I can arrange my own social life, thank you.'

'You are free to go,' Felipe replied, 'as long as you don't stay out too late. We need to make an early start in the morning.'

'That's settled, then,' Carlos sounded pleased.

Felipe raised a sardonic eyebrow before strolling out on to the terrace.

'I won't go if you think it's . . . inappropriate?' Evie cast around for the right word as she followed Felipe on to the terrace.

For some reason her heart was thumping at double its normal rate. Felipe looked up from the trade journal he was studying.

'I am annoyed,' he admitted, 'but only because I did not think to ask you first. Have a good time.'

Evie blinked at Felipe not sure she had heard him correctly. The net curtains stirred behind her and she suspected that yet again Catherine was eavesdropping.

★ ★ ★

The square was busy with brightly lit stalls selling local wine and flowers. A fish stew steamed in a huge wok for those who wished to partake of an early supper.

'I would prefer to eat later,' Carlos said, 'unless you are hungry?'

'I had tea,' Evie said, 'so I can wait.'

'The world-famous English tea.' Carlos smiled.

He looked extremely handsome in his open-necked white shirt and black dress trousers that looked as though they had been pressed to within an inch of their lives. He paused by a stall and purchased a red rose.

'For your hair,' he explained. 'Would you like me to place it for you?'

Glad she had worn her floaty floral skirt and a matching pink top that complemented his evening wear, Evie had allowed Carlos to link arms with her as together they had wandered through the stalls admiring the goods on display.

The ballet was scheduled to start at eight and the audience was seated under a huge canopy. Carlos had a colourful fan for Evie from one of the attendants.

'You will need it,' he insisted. 'Even though we are outside, the atmosphere can become stuffy.'

Evie watched the performance, entranced by the magic of a ballet she had always loved.

'Did you enjoy that?' Carlos asked as the cast took their final bows and the audience rose to its feet to applaud the company. There was a shower of red as roses were tossed on to the stage.

'It was wonderful,' Evie said as the ovation finally died down.

'Right, now I am really hungry,' Carlos looked at his watch. 'I have booked a table at Don Pedro's. We don't want to be late. The seafood paella is to die for.'

Seated outside with a wonderful view of the harbour, Evie ate glistening black olives and leaned back with a happy sigh.

'Tell me about yourself,' Carlos invited.

Evie was half prepared for such a question and had rehearsed what she was going to say. Briefly she explained that her father was Portuguese and that her parents now lived in the Azores running specialist breaks for wildlife enthusiasts.

'My father doesn't like the English weather, so my parents decided to move somewhere sunnier.'

'You did not want to go with them?'

'I was involved with someone at the time.'

Evie realised in surprise that it had been a while since she had thought about Duncan.

'It didn't work out.'

'I'm sorry,' Carlos sympathised.

Evie sipped her sparkling wine. Her self confidence had taken a serious dip when Duncan had broken things off between them to marry one of her friends but she was pleased he'd had the foresight to realise they weren't right for each other.

'Now it's your turn,' she said, recovering her composure.

'You know all there is to know about me. My father was a notary. When he retired I stepped into his shoes.'

'Have you always represented the Vicente family?'

'Yes.' Carlos nodded as two plates of steaming paella arrived at their table.

'*Bom appetite*,' the waiter said after twirling an enormous pepper mill over their food.

'How well do you know Astra?' Evie asked as she forked up a mouthful of rice.

'She has been a part of Marina for as long as anyone can remember. Of course I was not born when she first arrived but I remember my father mentioning how annoyed Eduardo's father was when Mauricio married her. He insisted his brother be cut off without a penny.'

'Could he do that?' Evie forked up some more paella.

'Antonio, Mauricio's brother, was the favourite son so he got his way. My father did not like Antonio and tried to persuade Senhor Vicente to change his mind but the old man was stubborn.

'Money was tight for Astra and Mauricio. Mauricio was reduced to taxiing the jet set around. He made some money doing odd jobs, helping out the fishermen, that sort of thing. It used to annoy my father because Antonio's side of the family were spendthrifts and liked the high life. The inheritance they had contrived to get from Senhor Vicente senior was soon squandered.'

'When did Felipe come to live with Astra and Mauricio?'

Carlos put down his fork.

'That's another unhappy story. Cassandra, Astra's daughter, also liked the high life. Marina did not hold enough excitement for her. She had seen the yachts down in the harbour and the people sunbathing on them. It used to annoy her that her parents had no money.

'She began going around with some of the rich kids, the summer visitors. Astra and Mauricio tried to keep an eye on her and forbade her from seeing one particular boy. I can't remember his name but he was a bad lot. One night Cassandra was confined to her room for some misdemeanour but she managed to break out and run off with him. It was a terrible scandal.

'Astra tried to use her influence to get her daughter back but by the time they caught up with her she was married.

'The tension eased a bit when Felipe was born but Cassandra was not the maternal type. She left Felipe in Astra's care while she and her husband carried on enjoying their parties.

'One day when they were travelling

from Italy to Monaco in one of their powerful cars there was an accident. No-one really knew what happened. Cassandra's husband liked driving fast cars and that stretch of road is very dangerous. That's all I can tell you. From that day Astra devoted her life to bringing up her grandson.'

'How sad.'

'As he grew older Mauricio became less happy with his lot. He never really bonded with Cassandra or Felipe and then after Antonio died his son Eduardo started to make a nuisance of himself. He wanted the castelo.'

'I've met Eduardo,' Evie said.

'When?' Carlos asked.

'Yesterday.'

'What did you think of him?'

'Family politics are none of my business but I didn't like him.'

'Let us talk of more pleasant topics.' Carlos smiled. 'Would you like a dessert? The ice-cream here is delicious. They flavour it with honey and almonds. You have to try it.'

Not wanting to disappoint Carlos but at the same time wondering how she was going to manage to eat another mouthful, Evie smiled her acceptance.

'We can always jog back to the castelo,' she joked, 'to work it off.'

'Tell me,' Carlos invited, 'how do you get on with Catherine? She seemed very keen for you to accept my invitation.'

'For some reason I think she has taken against me,' Evie admitted. 'She suspects I'm intent on making off with some of Astra's things.'

'Did you know she is Mauricio and Antonio's cousin?'

'No, I didn't.'

'That is why she is so fiercely protective of the family. They looked after her when she lost her husband at a young age. Have you met Olivia, Catherine's daughter?'

'I didn't know she had a daughter.'

'Catherine would like Olivia to marry Felipe. She probably sees you as a complication.'

'Me?'

'Felipe is an attractive man. The two of you have been thrown together through circumstances outside Catherine's control. She will not like that. The relationship will interfere with her plans.'

'My relationship with Felipe Periera is purely on a business basis.'

Carlos shrugged.

'That's not how Catherine would see it.'

'Olivia need not have any concerns on my account.'

'It does not matter. Olivia is dedicated to her career. She is in the legal profession too and the last time we met up she told me her work was her life.' A sad smile crossed Carlos's face.

'We used to play together as children and we went out together once or twice but she is very ambitious. I am only a small town notary. Olivia is a high flyer.'

With a dreamy look in his eyes, Carlos looked out across the harbour.

'People are making their way home,' he said, waving to some acquaintances.

'Perhaps we had better follow their

example. Now I've signed Felipe's contract I need to get down to work,' Evie replied, 'and I've been told I have an early start in the morning.'

Carlos signalled for the bill.

'No, no, I insist,' he said when Evie offered a contribution.

'But you paid for the tickets for the ballet and dinner.'

'It was my pleasure and as a proud Portuguese I cannot accept your kind offer.'

'In that case I hope you will allow me to treat you to a meal perhaps one evening?'

'We'll think about it,' Carlos said, signing the receipt, 'but I am glad you are suggesting another date. Marina comes to life in April after the winter's rest. There will be lots of things to do. You are not too tired to stroll back to the castelo or would you prefer a taxi?'

'It's such a lovely night, let's walk.'

'Someone has left a light on for you,' Carlos said as his lips brushed Evie's cheek.

With a brief wave, Carlos started back down the hill. Evie turned to face the castelo.

The memory of her arrival was still fresh in her mind, when Catherine had abruptly closed the front door in her face. This time it swung open before she had a chance to turn the handle. She stepped back, shielding her eyes against the shaft of light temporarily blinding her.

Felipe stepped out of the shadows to confront her.

'It's Astra,' he said.

Roses and Moonlight

'What's happened?' Evie demanded, her stomach churning.

'She felt unwell after you and Carlos left.' Felipe lapsed into silence as if uncertain how to continue.

Biting down her frustration, Evie took a deep breath. Felipe did not look in the mood to be hurried.

'And?' she coaxed in as gentle a voice as she could manage.

'I suspect things haven't been right for a while,' Felipe sounded as if he were speaking to himself. He gave a shaky smile. 'But I could never say anything. My grandmother is of a generation that gets on with things.'

Evie nodded, indicating she understood.

'She looked more tired than usual over supper and I was about to suggest she had an early night, then she dropped a plate and that seemed to distress her.

'Catherine said it wasn't the first time that something like this had happened. She told me she had been growing concerned about Astra but that my grandmother had forbidden her to say anything to me. I took the decision to call the doctor.'

There was none of the proud Portuguese about Felipe now. It was as if he were looking to Evie for reassurance that he had done the right thing.

'Felipe,' Evie moved towards him and touched his arm, 'I'm so sorry. You should have called me back.'

'It was better that you weren't here. Astra,' he paused, 'wasn't herself. When she found out that the doctor was coming she said things . . . ' He shrugged. 'You don't need to hear what she said but that's when I knew something was wrong. Astra is one of the kindest people in the world and I'm not just saying that because she is my grandmother. She has never raised her voice to me before — ever,' he emphasised.

'I believe you,' Evie said.

Felipe didn't appear to hear.

'I was glad she calmed down by the time the doctor arrived. He carried out a few basic tests then arranged for a private ambulance to take her to the local hospital. Catherine went with her and she has just telephoned to say they've decided to keep her in overnight.'

'You didn't go with your grandmother?'

'Catherine volunteered and Astra raised no objection. I thought it might be better given the circumstances.'

'What happens now?' Evie asked as Felipe lapsed back into silence.

'The doctor said they would carry out further tests and let me know.'

'Then you won't want me here, will you?'

Felipe looked surprised by Evie's question.

'I'd like you to stay until we know more about what is happening. Please?' he pleaded with a hopeful look.

'Wouldn't I be in the way?'

'Not at all — that's if you don't mind being here on your own. The castelo can be a lonely place when there's no-one else about.'

Felipe sounded as though he spoke from experience and that possibly the castelo did not hold the happiest of memories for him.

'You can carry on with the catalogue plans. I won't interfere. I'll even try to help when I can but I may not be around all that much.'

'If you're sure . . . '

'It's what Astra would have wanted and I do, too,' he added.

'Where is Catherine now?'

'She decided to go home to her villa in the village. That's why I was waiting up for you.'

'I wondered why the lights were still on,' Evie said, relieved she hadn't accused Felipe of spying on her and Carlos.

'I didn't want you waking up in the morning without knowing what had happened. I know you and Catherine don't exactly see eye to eye so I wanted to be the one to tell you.'

'Thank you,' Evie said touched by Felipe's concern.

He glanced at the rose that Carlos had placed in her hair.

'Did you have a good evening?' he asked.

Feeling embarrassed, Evie removed the flower. It seemed frivolous to tell Felipe about the ballet and the fish paella. Evie flushed with shame as she remembered how she had pumped Carlos for information about the Vicentes.

'I see you found Carlos good company,' Felipe said, mistaking the reason for Evie's heightened colour.

'He knows a lot of people.' She stumbled over her reply. 'And the festa was very busy.'

'I'm sorry I missed it. Would you like to join me in a nightcap?' he suddenly added.

Evie followed him out to the terrace. The table was littered with the remains of an abandoned supper. Felipe poured out two glasses of wine then cut himself a slice of bread and a hunk of cheese and quartered a fresh fig.

The glow from the patio heater created welcome warmth as the heat had now left the day. The fairy lights strung over the canopy twinkled in accompaniment to the background music coming from the festa.

'I think the celebrations will go on until late,' Felipe said, 'if past years are anything to go by. I hope it won't keep you awake.'

'There's not much that keeps me awake,' Evie assured him, surprised at the warm glow of Felipe's acknowledging smile.

'I am pleased to hear it. Would you like some cheese?' He nudged the plate towards her.

'I don't normally eat dessert but Carlos made me try some honey and almond ice-cream.'

'Delicious but filling? I can never resist it — even though I usually regret it afterwards.'

The fairy lights emphasised Felipe's chiselled features. He had the suntanned complexion of a man used to spending his time in the open air. Evie frowned. There was something else about him that reminded her of someone else.

'Now what shall we talk about?' he invited as he finished his supper. 'That's if you're not too tired?'

'Don't you have an early start in the morning?'

Evie wasn't sure she wanted to sit up late talking to such a dangerously attractive man, one she had every reason to mistrust.

'We keep late hours in Portugal, later I think than in your country?'

'You could tell me about your work,' Evie prompted, surprised to realise that despite her full day she didn't feel in the least tired and Felipe seemed in the mood to talk.

'I could,' Felipe acknowledged, 'but

why don't you ask me some questions, you know, like an interview? Go on,' he urged, 'think of something no-one's ever asked me before.'

For a second Evie's mind went blank. What question could she ask that Felipe hadn't heard a hundred times before? Then taking a deep breath she plunged in.

'Very few people know of your relationship to Astra Dempsey. Why?'

From the expression on Felipe's face Evie feared she might have touched a delicate spot.

'You don't have to answer if you don't want to,' she said.

'My grandmother means the world to me,' Felipe said in a quiet voice, 'and when she retired to Portugal she left her former life behind. She does not like publicity and I do not wish to trade on the connection.'

'Then what about the Vicente family? They have quite a history too but you rarely mention your connection to them.'

'You forget I am a Periera. I do not carry the Vicente family name.'

Emboldened by the glass of wine Felipe had urged on her, Evie pressed on.

'Your grandfather was a Vicente.'

'Agreed, but again that is nothing to do with my work.'

'You told me to make my questions interesting,' Evie persisted.

'I cannot deny that,' Felipe agreed. 'I do not mention the Vicente family because I want my work to speak for itself. The Vicentes invested in vineyards and local industries but now there is nothing left apart from the castelo which Eduardo claims is his inheritance and he is probably right. I would not wish to occupy the castelo against his will. So there you have it. Eventually my Vicente connection will be severed.'

The lights in the harbour were dimming but Felipe showed no sign of wanting the evening to end.

'What about you?' he asked.

Evie realised she had laid herself

open for cross-examination.

'My family history could be of no interest to you.'

'On the contrary. You have a Portuguese connection.' Felipe's eyes narrowed. 'Quinta? The name seems familiar to me.'

'Does it?' Evie affected a nonchalance she was far from feeling.

'Does your father come from this area?'

'He left Portugal when I was young.' Evie spoke quickly, avoiding a direct answer, then glanced at her watch. 'You said you had an early start in the morning.'

With her heart thumping so loudly she was amazed Felipe could not hear it, Evie straightened her shawl. He stood behind her chair as she got to her feet.

'You forgot your rose.' Felipe picked it up off the table.

The night air accentuated its scent as he held it towards her face. Evie blinked. Their fingers touched as he passed it over. His hand still raised, Felipe stroked her cheek with the pad of his thumb.

'Sleep well,' he said in a soft voice that set Evie's spine tingling.

On unsteady legs she made her way upstairs to bed.

A New Friend

The sun was high in the sky when Evie awoke the next day. Glancing at the clock, she saw to her horror it was past 10 o'clock. Despite what she'd told Felipe, she had found it difficult to fall asleep — not from the noise of the festa but from the memory of the touch of his hand on her face.

Determinedly dismissing thoughts of roses and moonlight, Evie quickly showered and dressed then opened her bedroom door.

'Hello,' a woman greeted her with a smile. 'Sorry, I didn't mean to make you jump. There is no need to look guilty unless what my mother has been saying about you is true.'

'Your mother?' A confused frown wrinkled Evie's brow.

'You are Evie?'

She nodded.

'I am Olivia, Catherine's daughter.'

'Oh,' was all Evie could manage to say.

'Exactly,' Olivia acknowledged a wry smile twisting her lips. 'My mother tells me you are keen to replace me in Felipe's affections, but you do not need to worry about me. I am not interested in marrying Felipe, despite my mother's best attempts to pair us up for life, so feel free to enjoy his company as much as you like. He's very good at football, by the way, at least he was fifteen or so years ago.'

'I'm sorry?' Evie was still confused.

'Poor you,' Olivia sympathised. 'I understand you had a late night and you've only just woken up and here I am going on about Felipe and football. Come on down and I'll get some coffee on the go, then we can get to know each other properly. How does that sound?'

Olivia was dressed in casual crops and a blue polo-necked sweater. Evie caught a whiff of an expensive French perfume as she followed her down to the kitchen.

'We're not normally allowed in here,' she confided, 'but as my mother is out who's to know? I won't tell if you won't.'

'Where is Catherine?'

'She and Felipe have gone to the hospital.'

'Is there any news on Astra?'

'Not yet, but I gather she had a quiet night.'

'Did Felipe leave a message for me?'

''Fraid not. How do you like your coffee? Strong and black?'

With the percolator bubbling comfortably Olivia sat down opposite Evie.

'While you're getting your head together I could tell you a bit about myself?' she suggested.

'Go ahead.' Evie blinked herself fully awake.

'I've known Astra all my life. She was good to me when I was growing up. She was like an honorary grandmother. I used to play with Felipe and we would do all the usual things together, play football, swim, ride, Felipe even took me to the school leavers' ball. I was never made to feel like I was the poor relation.'

'Your mother is related to the Vicentes, isn't she?' Evie asked.

'That's right. Mauricio was a second or third cousin — a relationship sufficiently removed for my mother to feel it was all right if I wanted to marry Felipe, only I don't. We're friends but that's as far as it goes.

'Anyway, my mother telephoned me last night to say Astra was unwell and that neither she nor Astra had seen me for a long time. She played the guilt trip card on me, so as I am due some leave I came straight home. I work in Faro,' she explained, 'in the legal profession.'

'I see,' was all Evie could think of to say.

Olivia poured out two mugs of piping hot coffee and looked through the window.

'It's windy out there this morning. Let's stay in here.' She sat down again. 'The reason I am not interested in

Felipe,' she confided to Evie, 'is because there's someone else.' She paused for dramatic effect. 'Carlos Diego.'

Evie coughed on a too hot mouthful of coffee.

'Sorry, went down the wrong way,' she croaked. 'Go on.'

'Carlos is the local notary.'

'I know,' Evie said, recovering her power of speech.

'Have you met him?'

Evie gave her coffee a vigorous stir then, anxious to avoid any further misunderstandings, she confessed.

'I went to the festa with him last night.'

'Did you indeed?' Olivia subjected her to a look of such intense scrutiny Evie feared she might have alienated her new and possibly only friend at the castelo.

'He seems to think you're a high flyer.'

'You talked about me?'

'Only briefly.'

'I was guilty as charged, I suppose,

but lately my values have changed. I'm missing Marina even though a few years ago I couldn't wait to leave. How did you meet Carlos?'

'I was out jogging one morning and I bumped into him.'

'Carlos jogging?'

'He's on a fitness regime.'

'I'm pleased to hear it. He could do with losing a kilo or two.'

'I had no idea who he was until Felipe suggested drafting a contract for me to sign before I started work here. Carlos turned up at the house with the finished draft and that's when I realised who he was.'

'My mother was telling me about the proposed catalogue of Astra's fashion collection.'

'Actually I should be working on it now.'

'There's no rush,' Olivia insisted. 'If you like I'll help you. I've nothing else to do and I'm sure I don't need a contract to work here,' she added with an impish smile. 'Why did you need one?'

'Promise you won't take this the wrong way?' Evie felt another surge of anxiety.

'Go on.'

'Your mother seems to think I'm some sort of spy. She wouldn't let me through the door when I first arrived. Apparently Astra hadn't told her of her plans and she took me for paparazzo. She shut the door in my face.'

Olivia broke into a peal of laughter.

'Poor you. I hope you will be gracious enough to accept my apology on behalf of the Emmanuel family?'

'Apology accepted,' Evie said, warming to Catherine's daughter.

'Once you were through the door how did you get on with Felipe?'

'Not much better.'

'He can be prickly with people he doesn't know.'

'But last night was different.'

'I thought you went out with Carlos last night.'

'Felipe was waiting up for me when I got back, to tell me about Astra,' Evie explained.

'I see.'

'We had a drink on the terrace while he finished his supper.'

'And your feelings for Felipe deepened over the *pastéis de nata*?' An impish smile curved the corner of Olivia's mouth.

'It wasn't like that,' Evie objected.

'Then how was it?'

'I saw a different side to him.'

She had dropped Carlos's red rose on her bedside cabinet, a crushed reminder of all that had happened the previous evening. If she closed her eyes she could still smell its sweet perfume. Then, aware of Olivia's scrutiny, Evie went on.

'Felipe gave me the impression he wasn't happy at the castelo as a child.'

Olivia sipped her coffee.

'He never really bonded with his grandfather. Mauricio was quite strict with Felipe. Astra was always making excuses for his behaviour.'

'What sort of excuses?'

'Felipe will probably kill me for

telling you this but for a while he went off the rails — nothing too serious but enough to cause his grandparents to be concerned. He played around with the fast crowd.

'Those friends had influential parents to get them out of trouble but Mauricio refused to help Felipe and in the end he was sent away.'

'To prison?' Evie was horrified.

Olivia broke into another of her spontaneous laughs.

'To boarding school, in England. Astra tried to protest but Mauricio would not be swayed. I missed him badly but the discipline was what Felipe needed.

'When he came back he had grown up a lot and he became a much nicer person. He developed an interest in photography and well . . . you know the rest. Is that the telephone?' Olivia cocked an ear. She left Evie to finish her coffee while she answered it.

'That was my mother,' Olivia came back into the kitchen. 'Astra is being difficult and insisting on coming home. Felipe's been called away to a meeting so I've got to go and fetch them. Will you be all right here until we get back?'

'I'll be fine,' Evie assured her. 'I'll make a start on things in the attic.'

'Good idea. I shouldn't linger here. This is my mother's domain and from what you've told me you've already chalked up more than your fair share of black marks.'

Evie waved Olivia off then returning to the kitchen rinsed the mugs and left them to drain. The sound of footsteps on the terrace alerted her to the arrival of a visitor.

'Hello?' she called out then, receiving no reply, she went to investigate.

Eduardo was lounging on Astra's sun bed. He greeted Evie with an unpleasant smile.

'There you are,' he said.

'Everyone's out,' she informed him.

'Was that Olivia Emmanuel I saw driving away?' he asked.

'She's gone to collect Catherine from

the hospital. Astra was admitted last night.'

'Had another of her funny turns, has she?'

'She was feeling unwell, yes.'

Evie wished Eduardo would leave but without being rude there was nothing she could do. He had more right to be here than she did.

'No matter,' Eduardo said with a disinterested shrug. 'It's you I want to talk to and it's better we have this conversation when there's no-one else around to overhear what I have to say.'

'I don't understand.'

'I think you do,' Eduardo sneered. 'Don't play the innocent with me. I find it insulting to my intelligence.'

Evie decided it was not the time for good manners and, visitor or not, Eduardo had outstayed his welcome.

'I think you had better leave.'

'I'm not going anywhere until I've had my say. I thought the name Quinta rang a bell so I did a little research.' He paused for dramatic effect. 'You're that troublemaker Francisco's daughter, aren't you? Don't bother denying it, you would be wasting your time.'

'What do you want?' Evie demanded.

'You came here to exact revenge on the family, didn't you?'

'I came here at Astra's request.'

'It must have been very convenient for you when this little job came up. Well, I've another little job for you.'

'I'm already fully employed.'

'You can't afford to turn down my offer.'

'Whatever it is, I'm not interested.'

'Then let me put it another way. If you don't help me I shall tell Felipe who you really are.'

A look of disgust crossed Evie's face.

'I'm not giving in to blackmail.' She tossed her head in a confident gesture of dismissal. 'Tell Felipe what you like.'

'What about Astra? Her health may not be up to it if she knows you're the daughter of the man who bankrupted the family.'

'You wouldn't?' Evie gasped.

'I'd do anything to get what I want.'

'What do you want?'

'The rights your father denied me. His silly threatened court case ate up the last of the family finances.'

'My father didn't ruin the family.'

'He stirred up a lot of unnecessary unrest,' Eduardo made a gesture of distaste, 'but that is not the reason I am here. Listen to what I have to say.'

'I've heard enough.'

Evie turned away from him. In one swift movement Eduardo grabbed her arm, his fingers circling her wrist. She bit down a cry of pain.

'No-one has been allowed in that wretched attic for years. It's hiding a secret — I know it is — and I want to know what that secret is. Why do you think Felipe was reluctant to let you have a look round?'

'I've no idea.'

'He even posted Catherine on look-out. She's so indebted to the family she'll do anything for them.'

'I'm sorry to disappoint you. There's

nothing in the attic but dresses and memorabilia from Astra's modelling days.'

Evie tried to struggle free but Eduardo's hold on her wrist was too strong.

'My father suspected that Mauricio and Astra were never married.'

'That's a ridiculous accusation.'

'I'm inclined to agree with you, but if it is true then I am the heir to the castelo. You are in a perfect position to have a good snoop.'

'What am I supposed to be looking for?'

'Written evidence? Certificates, something of that nature.'

Evie was fast losing patience with him.

'How can I possibly prove someone wasn't married? There would be no certificate and if you want evidence of a marriage then try the public records office.'

'I have to know if Cassandra was born out of wedlock. Unfortunately my father and Mauricio fell out so badly they didn't speak to each other for years. I have no idea when my cousin was born and I can find no record of the birth of Cassandra Dempsey or a Cassandra Vicente anywhere.'

'Then I can't help.'

'You will help me.'

'I don't give in to bullies.'

'You'll regret this,' Eduardo snarled.

'Maybe I will, but even if you expose my past to Felipe, you still won't get your wretched evidence, will you? Now if you'll excuse me, I think I hear a car.'

'You haven't heard the last of this.'

Eduardo towered over Evie, his eyes glittering with anger. Shaking but determined not to show any weakness, Evie glared back at him. For a moment she thought he might go as far as striking her but the sound of voices caused him to recoil, then hurry off down the path leading to the harbour.

'Was that Eduardo I saw talking to you?' Catherine asked Evie, her eyes not missing a thing.

'He called by but he couldn't stay,' Evie admitted.

'What did he want?'

'Evie, darling,' Astra looked pale but her smile was as bright as ever, 'such a nuisance all this. I don't know why Felipe made such a fuss. I'm very annoyed with him. Catherine, your arm please — and Olivia, why don't you and Evie make a start on the attic? We must be so behind schedule.'

'Come on, partner.' Olivia linked arms with Evie. 'Let's go see what we can find in the holy of holies.'

A Startling Revelation

'What was Eduardo doing here?' Olivia asked as she unlocked the attic door.

'He told me something about Mauricio and Astra not being married.'

'That old tale!' Olivia laughed as she shook out a velvet evening dress and put it on a padded hanger. 'Eduardo has been trying to flog it for years. Mauricio and Astra were married all right. That's why poor old Mauricio was disinherited.

'His father never accepted Astra or their daughter Cassandra and he refused to acknowledge them, even on his deathbed.' She raised her eyes. 'Families. At least Mauricio and Astra were happy although Cassandra gave them a lot of grief.'

'Do you know when Cassandra was born?' Evie asked, photographing the velvet dress.

'No idea. Is it important?' Olivia paused.

'I'm not sure. It was something Eduardo said.'

'He hasn't been threatening you, has he? He can be a bully.'

'He wanted me to poke around up here to see what I could find out,' Evie admitted.

'I hope you told him no deal.'

'I did and he wasn't best pleased.'

'Eduardo is like his father — not a nice person. He wants to sell the castelo and take the money.'

'He can't do that, can he?'

'I have no idea but what sort of man would throw his elderly aunt out of the family home for the sake of money?'

Before Evie could reply she heard Catherine's voice calling up the stairs.

'Carlos is here to see you, Senhorita Evie. You'd better come down. Senhor Felipe does not like you being up there on your own and it is difficult for me to climb the stairs.'

'I'm up here too, *Mãe*,' Olivia called

down, pulling a face at Evie. 'You needn't worry. I'm keeping an eye on things and with Carlos here too I'm sure nothing will go missing.'

'Best do as your mother says,' Evie advised.

Gently closing the lid to the trunk, Evie switched off the light and followed Olivia down the narrow staircase. Carlos was waiting at the foot of the stairs, an eager smile on his face.

'Olivia,' he greeted her. 'I did not know you were here.'

'It's good to see you,' Olivia replied.

To Evie's amusement she blushed as Carlos kissed her on both cheeks.

'You have come to invite Senhorita Evie out to dinner?' Catherine interrupted the exchange.

'Sorry,' Evie was quick to decline, 'I have to update my boss in England. I haven't been in touch for a day or so. Why don't you take Olivia out instead, Carlos?' she suggested. 'You can catch up on old times.'

Knowing she had been outwitted,

Catherine muttered her way back down the stairs.

'If you'll excuse me?' Evie eased past Carlos and Olivia and padded along the landing back to her room.

'Where have you been?' Lesli demanded as Evie logged on. 'I've been trying to get hold of you for days.'

'Don't exaggerate,' Evie said, well used to Lesli playing the drama queen.

'Well, maybe not days,' Lesli conceded. 'What have you got to tell me? Have you signed your contract?'

'I have.'

'Then is it all systems go?'

'Not quite. Astra's been unwell so I haven't made as much progress as I would have liked.'

'What's wrong with her?'

'She's been having tests.'

'That could mean anything. Where is she now?'

'Back at the castelo.'

'Do we still have the green light?'

'I think so. I've been working on the collection this afternoon with Olivia.'

'Who's she?'

'Catherine's daughter, the family retainer I told you about?'

'Right.'

Evie could sense Lesli's attention wandering.

'Did you find out anything about Shaun Merrony?' she asked.

'Did I not?' Lesli looked re-animated. 'Apparently he and Astra hung out together for a while. There was even a rumour that they were engaged but nothing ever came of it. He was the one who took the famous tiger picture.'

'Was he indeed?' Evie was intrigued.

'It was his best piece of work.'

'Why didn't he capitalise on it?'

'Stop interrupting.'

'Sorry.'

'I'm coming to the best bit. Shaun's parents were American society and we are talking serious society. Mr Merrony senior was a diplomat. They moved in the highest social circles. Get the picture?'

Evie nodded.

'They wouldn't have approved of Shaun's

involvement with Astra. I expect they had someone else in mind for him — probably the daughter of an old family friend.'

'Shaun and Astra?' Evie prompted, not really interested in the Merrony family's social position.

'Right. I think they kept their relationship under wraps because of Shaun's background. Anyway, the Merronys always held an annual midsummer party at their country pad in Dorset. The date coincided with Mrs Merrony's birthday so it was a good opportunity to get the gang together.'

'If the Merronys were American, what were they doing living in Dorset?'

'They had the use of this mansion or something. Anyway, the midsummer party — the story goes that Astra didn't attend because she was unwell. I think Shaun was going to seize the opportunity to introduce her to his folks but Astra threw a sickie probably because she couldn't face his parents and from what I've heard about them I can't say I blame her.

'Only the best would do for their son and Astra was not their idea of a suitable life companion for Shaun.'

'Poor Astra. She's still got a photo of Shaun, you know.'

'Are you sure? He was notoriously camera shy.'

'She showed it to me. I suspect she might still be in love with him. You know the first love, the one you can't forget?'

'Stop sounding so soppy.' There was a note of disgust in Lesli's voice. 'Anyway, I haven't finished.' Lesli raised her voice. 'The midsummer party went on all night. No-one realised Shaun was missing until breakfast the next morning. A search was made for him. He was found in the swimming pool. It was assumed he had dived in and hit his head. The affair was hushed up because his father pulled diplomatic strings.'

'You mean he died?' Evie was no longer smiling.

'Sad, isn't it?'

'What happened then?'

'That's where I came up against a brick wall. Although it's unofficial it's generally accepted that Shaun's death was the reason Astra quit the modelling scene and fled to Portugal.'

'How did you find all this out?'

'I had to call in several favours.'

'Surely news of Shaun's death would have leaked out?'

'It did, of course, but the potential scandal was played down. Things were different in the Sixties. It was easier to keep things under wraps. These days it would be out there almost before it happened.'

'And Astra never breathed a word of their supposed engagement to anyone?'

'Nope, at least I don't think so. The Merronys probably wouldn't have believed her and she had no claim on their son.'

'How can people behave like that?'

'The world was a different place then. People were still class conscious, I suppose.'

'I'm glad we've moved on.'

'Talking of moving on, you'd best get

on with the job in hand and come home as soon as possible,' Lesli advised. 'If the press get a sniff of Astra's state of health it might re-ignite interest in her career. The Sixties are red hot right now. There's a lot of retro stuff going on.'

'Things should be easier now I've signed Felipe's contract.'

'What's the grandson like?'

'He's good,' Evie said without much conviction.

'Like that, is it?'

'I don't know what you mean.' Evie did her best to sound casual.

'Hmm, well, don't you go falling in love with some handsome Spaniard.'

'Felipe is Portuguese.'

'Same thing.'

'I shouldn't let Felipe hear you say that,' Evie said. 'The Portuguese are proud of their heritage.'

'Never mind.' Lesli flapped her hands. 'If you find out anything else that you think I ought to know don't leave me out of the loop. Ciao.'

Lesli cut the call, leaving a thoughtful Evie wondering exactly what had gone on between Astra and Shaun. Was his death the reason Astra had fled the country?

She hadn't been at the party so there was no way she could have been involved in what had happened but within the year she was involved with Mauricio and she never returned home, that much Evie knew.

With a sigh, she returned her attention to her notes. The photos she had taken were not as good as those taken by Felipe but she couldn't hang around and wait for him to find some spare time to help.

As for Astra, she was fickle and Evie feared she might change her mind and cancel the project.

'We're off out now.' Olivia poked her head round Evie's door. 'Sure you won't join us?'

'I'd best get on with some paper-work.' Evie smiled back at her. 'Have a good time.'

Reluctant to go back up to the attic on her own, Evie wrote up her notes and annotated the photos. Despite the frequent interruptions, the collection was coming along surprisingly well and two hours later Evie sat back with a satisfied sigh as she inspected her work.

'There you are.' Felipe now stood in the doorway. 'I've sent Catherine home. I told her I would keep an eye on Astra and with you here to keep me company there was no need for her to worry about anything.' He paused. 'Catherine's very annoyed with you, by the way. What have you done now?' he enquired.

Evie answered with a rueful smile.

'I sent Olivia out to dinner with Carlos.'

'Why has that upset Catherine?' Felipe looked mildly interested.

'You don't know?'

'Perhaps you'd enlighten me.'

'Olivia and Carlos?'

'Carlos is a nice guy. What's wrong with him and Olivia getting together?'

'I don't know that Catherine agrees with you. She has other ideas. Anyway she saw me as a suitable diversion in the love triangle.'

'All this is beyond me,' Felipe replied dismissively, leaving Evie glad she wasn't going to have to go into further explanations. 'Have you had supper?'

'I hadn't thought about it,' Evie admitted.

'In that case you must let me cook for you this evening.'

'What about Astra?'

'She's asleep. Do you like,' he paused, 'I think the English translation is tuna fish?'

'Yes,' Evie replied.

'Then I will prepare our local speciality. We serve it with onions and tomato sauce, if you'd like to come down when you're ready?'

After a quick shower Evie dried her hair while she decided what to wear. She didn't want to look as though she had made a special effort for a casual supper date, but neither did she want

Felipe thinking she was over casual.

In the end she opted for one of her colourful T-shirts and her floral skirt. Grabbing her shawl she made her way downstairs to where Felipe was barbecuing their supper.

Like Evie he had gone for casual — a crisp white shirt and tailored dark chinos, but his smile was anything but casual. Evie faltered on the flagstones as he continued to smile.

'It's all ready,' he said. 'Why don't you make yourself comfortable while I serve?'

On the Brink of Confession

'I understand,' Felipe said, as he finished off the last of his tuna steak, 'that Eduardo paid you a visit?'

Evie gave a nervous smile.

'Who told you?' She suspected Catherine was the culprit.

'Is it true?' he demanded.

Evie nodded. Felipe leaned forward and before she realised his intention placed his hand over hers.

'No matter what,' he insisted, 'you must not let my uncle intimidate you.'

'He didn't,' Evie replied, crossing the fingers of her free hand under the table.

Felipe's dark brown eyes narrowed, full of doubt.

'You are not, I think, telling me the truth.'

Evie didn't trust herself to speak. She had never been good at fibbing and knew her guilt would be obvious by the expression on her face.

'You are hiding something from me,' Felipe persisted, picking up her body language. 'Is it to do with your family?'

'I don't know what you mean,' Evie retaliated quickly.

'I am not blind, Evie,' Felipe's face softened into a smile. 'You speak our language, your father was Portuguese. I suspect he came from this area. It stands to reason there is a connection with the Vicentes. Won't you tell me what it is that's bothering you and why Eduardo has been harassing you?'

The pleading tone in Felipe's voice was Evie's undoing. Perhaps it would be better to confess all now. That way Eduardo would have no ammunition to use against her and Felipe would know all there was to know about her family's past.

If he sent her home then she would have some explaining to do to Lesli but she'd cross that bridge when she came to it.

'Eduardo wasn't very pleasant to me,'

she began, choosing her words carefully.

'Why?' Felipe demanded.

Evie hesitated, wondering where to start, then took a deep breath but before she could speak they both heard a frantic ringing of Astra's bedside bell.

'My grandmother!' Felipe threw down his napkin and jumped to his feet, his chair crashing to the ground behind him. 'I told her only to ring in case of emergency.'

'I'll come with you,' Evie said and together they raced up the stairs.

'Where've you been?' Astra demanded petulantly.

'On the terrace, having supper with Evie,' Felipe replied. 'Are you unwell?'

'No.' Astra continued to pout.

'Then why did you ring?'

'I thought everyone had left me.' Astra looked like a sulky child. 'I do not like being on my own.'

'I would never leave you alone,' Felipe insisted. 'You know that.'

'I don't know anything any more.'

Astra still sounded querulous.

'Would you like some water?'

'I'd like a cup of coffee.'

'The doctor said caffeine would make it difficult for you to sleep, which is what you should be doing now, not ringing bells and upsetting everyone.'

'Pah!' Astra brushed aside her grandson's objection. 'Coffee,' she insisted.

Felipe cast Evie an imploring look.

'Why don't we all have a cup of decaff?' she suggested in a bright voice, hoping to diffuse the tension.

'Good idea,' Felipe said with a note of approval. 'One cup of coffee, then you go to sleep. Do we understand each other?'

'I suppose so,' Astra said, still sounding sulky. 'Off you go. Evie can keep me company and don't forget to bring up some of those lovely fruit marzipans we have and don't tell me I am forbidden to eat them. I helped Catherine make them.'

Raising his eyes in tolerant indulgence Felipe left the room.

Astra turned to Evie, all smiles again.

'That's got rid of him.' She still looked like a naughty child. 'Sit down and tell me how are you two getting on? Having supper together, were you?'

Astra's interruption had caused Evie's confession about her father's past history with the Vicente family to be lost. Not sure if she was relieved or not Evie smiled back at the older woman.

'We were on the terrace,' she admitted.

'Alone?'

'Catherine's not here, if that's what you mean,' Evie replied.

'You know why Catherine has taken against you?' Astra's deep green eyes were full of mischief. 'She thinks Felipe might fall in love with you.'

Evie tried hard not to flush.

'I am here to work,' she insisted.

'That never stopped anyone falling in love.' Astra dismissed Evie's objection with a wave of her hand. 'I think the two of you go well together. You have my blessing.'

'Astra, behave,' Evie chided. Despite her petulance it was hard to be cross with the older woman. Her sense of fun appealed to Evie.

Astra's smile widened.

'Shall I tell you something else?'

'If you like.' Evie wished Felipe would hurry up with the coffee.

'My real name is Aggie Backshaw.'

This was not what Evie had been expecting.

'Is it?' she said, trying not to look too surprised.

'I think that's why my father-in-law never took to me. I was hardly the choice of bride Raffelo would have wanted for his elder son. His wife Isabella was Spanish aristocracy. There were rumours she was related to the royal household. When Mauricio said he wanted to marry me Raffelo was scandalised. Did you know he disowned Mauricio?'

'I had heard,' Evie admitted.

'The daughter of a miner called Stan and a mother who worked in a shop was not what he would have wished for his son — worse still, I was English. If he'd been able to I'm sure Raffelo would have tried to have the marriage annulled.'

'How long were you married?' Evie enquired, briefly wondering if the story Eduardo had told her was true.

'I forget,' Astra replied airily.

'Were you married at the castelo?' Evie tried another tack.

There was a disturbance in the doorway.

'Here's Felipe with the coffee,' Astra greeted her grandson. 'Put it down there, darling. What treats have you brought us?' She inspected the tray with an eager smile.

'Some of Catherine's almond biscuits and her special marzipan fruits.'

'Perfect.' Astra leaned back against her pillow with a sigh.

Felipe poured the coffees and passed one over to Astra before turning to Evie.

'Sugar? Cream?' he asked.

'I'll take it black, thank you,' Evie replied.

'You won't sleep,' Astra admonished her.

'Then I'll do some work,' Evie said. 'There's a lot to get through,' she added.

'Sassy, aren't you?' Astra made a face.

'This collection was your idea,' Felipe reminded his grandmother.

'I'm not sure it was,' she replied.

'You're not going to pull out, are you?' Evie asked with a qualm of concern.

'Who knows?'

'Stop teasing Evie.' Felipe frowned. 'If you're wasting our time then let us know now before things go any further.'

'You're exactly like your grandfather,' Astra complained, nibbling a marzipan fruit, 'always complaining.'

'With due reason.'

'Hello?' a voice called up the stairs.

'Visitors at this time of night?' Astra raised her eyebrows.

139

'We're up here,' Felipe called down to Olivia and Carlos. 'Come and join us.'

'This is turning into a party.' Astra smiled. 'Felipe, get some more coffee cups.'

'Not for us,' Carlos insisted as he and Olivia poked their heads round the bedroom door, 'I have an early start in the morning.'

'Olivia,' Astra greeted her, 'I haven't had a chance to talk to you since you drove us back from the hospital. Have you been hiding from me?'

Olivia came forward and kissed her on the cheek.

'I don't think you are ill,' she teased. 'I think you are a fraud.'

'That's not true.'

From the expression on Astra's face it was clear she was enjoying being the centre of attention.

'I come home at my mother's express wish because she says you are not well and what do I find? You are having a party. You don't call that fraudulent?'

'Where have you been?' Astra cast a look in Carlos's direction.

'To Don Pedro's,' Carlos replied.

'Didn't you take Evie there last night?' Astra tried to look innocent but failed.

'Yes, and I know all about it,' Olivia butted in, 'so stop stirring things up.'

'I think,' Felipe said, picking up the empty coffee cups, 'that this party is over. Astra must rest and we all have work to do in the morning.'

'I'm helping Evie,' Olivia explained. 'May I stay overnight? If that's all right with everyone?'

'Of course it is,' Felipe replied.

'Will you want Olivia to sign one of Carlos's contracts,' Evie couldn't resist asking, 'before she's allowed back in the attic?'

'Olivia is family,' Felipe replied.

'You wish, at least I'm sure Catherine does,' Astra said with a stifled yawn.

Felipe cast his grandmother a stern look.

'Do you have everything you want?'

'Thank you, yes. You can all go now,' she said waving her hands in dismissal.

'She's impossible, isn't she?' Evie whispered as she and Olivia made their way down the stairs.

'I wouldn't have her any other way, would you?'

Evie had to admit that she wouldn't.

Ending in Tears

The following few days passed in a whirl of activity. Olivia proved a good assistant and the two girls worked well together. It was through Olivia that Evie learned more about the history of the Vicente family.

'Antonio was the blue-eyed boy,' she explained as they were going through Astra's collection of geometric prints. 'Look at this.' Distracted, Olivia held up a bold tangerine and scarlet garment. 'Is it a blouse or a dress?'

Evie held it up against herself and looked in the full-length mirror.

'I think it's fun and it's definitely a dress,' she said.

'No wonder old Raffelo disapproved of Astra. He was very strait-laced. Local legend has it he almost had a heart attack when she appeared on the scene.' Olivia returned her attention to sorting through more clothes. 'Astra certainly brought her entire collection with her when she moved here. It's as if she had made a mental decision never to return home.'

'You were telling me about Antonio,' Evie prompted.

'Hmm? Right.' Olivia jotted down a description of the dress in Evie's notebook. 'Antonio was the good-looking one. Poor old Mauricio could never compete with him. There was about eighteen months between them but they were worlds apart.

'Mauricio took after his father and Antonio was like Isabella. She died when the boys were young and I suppose Raffelo favoured Antonio because he reminded him of his wife.'

Evie thought back to her own childhood. She had no brothers or sisters but had never felt lonely and although her father missed his homeland she had felt happy and loved in the country he had adopted as his own.

She'd known little of his history with

the Vicentes but her mother had once let slip how she would never forgive the family for what they had done to her husband.

'Antonio never missed a chance to put Mauricio in a bad light and Mauricio played right into his hands by marrying Astra. Of course by then much of the family fortune had been dissipated. Lands had been sold off to pay for Antonio's extravagances.

'Isabella had brought with her a sizable dowry — family jewellery, properties, investments, but everything was forfeited to pay off the debts. The vineyards had to be sold off and soon there was nothing left, apart from the castelo. It's entailed to the family of the eldest son, but that hasn't stopped Eduardo wanting to get his hands on it.'

'Why does Eduardo think Mauricio and Astra weren't married?'

'There was some talk of Mauricio being engaged to a local girl. I don't know whether it's true or not. Her father had money and I think Raffelo had his eye on her fortune.'

'Who was Eduardo's mother?' Evie asked.

'Her name was Sofia. Marrying her was his one moment of madness but she was as greedy as Antonio. Together they ran through the family fortune then she died. I don't really know what happened but I think she's the reason Eduardo has never married.

'If there's any inheritance around I think he wants to keep it all to himself.' Olivia smiled. 'Felipe is the only good one of the bunch. He is so nice, don't you think?' She cast Evie a speculative look.

'I've already had this conversation with Astra,' Evie said firmly. 'Felipe is proud and Portuguese. I am English and from a much more humble background.'

'You are half Portuguese,' Olivia pointed out.

'That's as maybe, but like Astra I am from humble stock and I'm sure Felipe is not going to repeat the family mistake of marrying beneath him.'

'Whoa!' Olivia laughed. 'Who said anything about marriage?'

Evie tossed a blouse at Olivia.

'Catalogue,' she commanded. 'We haven't got all day.'

'Yes, ma'am.' Olivia mock saluted her.

'What was all that about marriage?' Felipe asked, stooping down as he entered the attic.

The amused look he cast Evie made her suspect he had heard most of the conversation. She flushed to the roots of her hair.

'Hello, Felipe,' Olivia greeted him. 'What are you doing up here?'

'I came to tell you your mother has gone home early.'

Olivia dropped the blouse she was holding.

'Is she unwell?'

'Astra is being tiresome and to be honest I think Catherine is exhausted.'

Olivia looked at Evie.

'Go,' Evie said. 'I can manage here.

We're nearly through. Thanks for all your help.'

'I'll run you down to the village if you like,' Felipe offered. 'Evie, would you mind keeping an eye on Astra for me? Hopefully she won't wake up while I'm out. I won't be long.'

Olivia clattered down the stairs after Felipe, leaving Evie alone in the attic. Apart from Astra she realised there was no-one else in the castelo.

Hesitantly, she moved towards an old bureau hidden away in a far corner. She'd never really noticed it before and she wondered why it was up here.

The roll top lid wasn't locked but it was difficult to open. After one or two hefty pushes it relented and opened wide enough to reveal empty shelves. There was nothing inside, not even a hidden recess or secret drawer containing long-lost family secrets.

With a feeling of relief, Evie closed the lid. Her work here was almost finished and Eduardo could do his worst. She wasn't going to pry into private family archives just because he wanted to get his hands on the castelo.

'Evie, is that you?' She heard Astra calling her name as she crept down the attic stairs.

'Coming,' Evie replied.

'I need a clean nightdress and my hair is an absolute mess and where's Catherine?'

Evie was still running around seeing to Astra's needs when Felipe returned.

'I will engage the services of a nurse,' he promised, his eyes taking in the situation at one glance.

'I don't want a nurse,' Astra complained. 'If Catherine is too ill to look after me then Evie can take on her duties.'

'Don't be difficult.'

For the first time since Evie had known him, Felipe came close to snapping at his grandmother. He gestured Evie to leave what she was doing and come outside.

'I'm sorry,' he apologised. 'I was away longer than I had envisaged.'

'How's Catherine?'

'She's been signed off with exhaustion. She does the work of three people and Astra is very demanding. I am going down to the agency to see about engaging a housekeeper. A nurse will also be with us tomorrow but I don't know what to do about tonight.'

Evie recognised his words for what they were — an appeal for help.

'We could do a split shift?' she suggested.

'I couldn't possibly impose on you,' Felipe said.

'I can manage one night,' Evie smiled. 'You arrange a housekeeper and I'll see to Astra.'

'Thank you,' he said.

Before Evie could respond he leaned forward cupped her chin in his hand and kissed her on the cheek.

'I'm glad you came. I don't know what I'd do without you.'

She did not move until she heard his car drive off down the hill towards the village.

'Read me some English news off your pad thing,' Astra said after Evie had settled her down. 'It's nice to hear a proper English accent, even if you're not from Newcastle.'

Her breathing became rhythmic as Evie recounted the lighter events of the week that she thought would interest Astra.

'A design college has held a fashion review,' Evie read out the details, 'and there's been a film premier in Leicester Square.'

'Not one of those time slip things, I hope.' Astra's voice made Evie jump. 'Try the book reviews.'

'Someone's written a tell-all exposé on a famous politician.' In desperation Evie swiped through her local headlines. 'They're holding an early Easter egg hunt near my neighbourhood park.'

'I've always loved chocolate,' Astra said, a look of pleasure on her tired face. 'Shaun and I used to eat it all the time, yet we were so thin in those days. Shaun would buy me huge boxes of Belgian chocolates and I thought nothing of scoffing them all in one session. The only time I couldn't face chocolate was when I was pregnant with Cassandra.'

'Do you want to talk about your daughter?' Evie asked in a soft voice but there was no reply from the bed. Astra had fallen asleep.

'Thank goodness for that.' Felipe arrived back shortly afterwards. 'I've arranged everything. The new housekeeper will start tomorrow and a nurse is scheduled to visit in the morning.' He glanced towards his grandmother. 'She looks very peaceful, doesn't she?'

'I've been reading snippets of news to her,' Evie indicated her iPad, 'and she fell asleep on me.'

'I'll sit with her tonight.' Felipe pulled out a chair. 'Why don't you rest up? You've had a busy day.'

'Can I get you something to eat?' Evie offered.

'Maybe a sandwich?'

'I'll see what I can find in the kitchen.'

Felipe joined her for a scratch supper on the small balcony that led off Astra's bedroom. The sun was sending out golden rays as it began its descent on the day and the flowers in the garden were giving off their evening scents. The smell revived more of Evie's childhood memories of evening suppers with her parents in the days before they had been forced to move.

'What are you thinking of?' Felipe asked as he filled her wine glass.

The dying sun cast shadows on the balcony and a feeling of unease crept up her spine.

'Did I say something to unsettle you?' Felipe looked concerned as Evie shivered.

'I was,' Evie paused, 'remembering the past.'

'Perhaps we should go back inside,' Felipe suggested. 'You look cold. Why don't you have an early night? Take a long hot bath and relax. It's what I do when things get on top of me.'

Following Felipe's advice Evie wallowed in the bath, soaping away the cares of the day before she fell into bed.

'Evie, wake up.'

She heard Felipe's urgent voice through a veil of sleep.

'What's the matter?' She rubbed a hand over her eyes as she tried to focus on what he was saying.

'It's Astra.'

Instantly alert, she sat up straight. Tears were trickling down Felipe's face and his eyes were red-rimmed from crying. He sank on to the edge of her bed. Evie put her arms around him as he laid his head on her shoulder, his body shaking with uncontrollable sobs.

Worst Fears . . .

'You will stay on, won't you?' Felipe begged Evie as news of Astra's death broke and the world's press descended on the castelo, besieging the village, even camping in the road outside, eager for a glimpse of anyone connected to the fashion icon of the 60s.

Astra's famous tiger photograph was displayed on all the television channels and the resurgence of interest in her career was phenomenal. Everyone was eager to know more about the recluse who had disappeared off the scene decades earlier at the height of her career.

'Surely it's Catherine's place to be here,' Evie said quietly. She had not expected to feel such grief for someone she had known for only a short time.

'Olivia tells me her mother isn't up to coming back and you know how she is with people she doesn't know. Someone could get hurt.'

They both knew Felipe was referring to the swarms of photographers outside. Their presence was clogging the narrow road leading to the castelo and making life difficult for the locals. Evie suspected it was Olivia's decision not to allow her mother to return to work and she thought it was a wise one.

Felipe ran a hand through his hair. It didn't look as though it had received any attention since his grandmother's death and there were dark circles under his eyes.

'I need someone I can rely on,' Felipe admitted. 'Please?'

'If you're sure?' Evie was still hesitant. Her heart was telling her to stay but her other senses were warning her against it.

Astra's death had revealed a side to Felipe she hadn't seen before, one she was growing to admire and respect, emotions she had to keep in check. He had dealt with the pressure without losing his cool and at times his patience must have been pushed to the limit.

Evie knew Felipe had turned to her for help because he was feeling vulnerable but she was under no illusions. When life returned to normal they would go their separate ways. Their lifestyles would not clash again.

She hoped now Felipe would never discover her family's connection to the Vicentes. Her own motivation for finding out the truth no longer seemed important.

'He needs you.' Carlos had added his weight to Felipe's request. 'We all do. You know how to deal politely with that rabble out there. The rest of us would probably say or do something we might regret. We're all on the point of losing it.'

'Can't you get them moved on?' Evie had pleaded as yet another news van drove up, disgorging more reporters all shouting loudly to each other. 'This is a house in mourning.'

'I'll try.' Carlos squeezed her elbow in

a gesture of sympathy. 'Perhaps I could try quoting infringement of the law at them. You never know, it might work.'

'What's going to happen now?' Evie asked.

The room they were in still displayed the vases of fresh flowers that Astra loved to pick every morning. It was as if she had only stepped outside for a few minutes and any moment Evie expected to hear her coming back.

'I don't know,' Carlos admitted.

'The castelo?'

He shrugged.

'It's not going to be easy sorting out Astra's affairs and I'm glad it's not my responsibility.' His eyes now rested on the grand piano in the corner of the day-room. Someone had draped it in a black cloth and placed a candlestick on top of it. Three ivory coloured candles had been placed in the holders but remained unlit. 'She made such a great impact on all our lives.' Carlos blinked rapidly as if embarrassed by his unmanly show of emotion. 'I don't see how things can continue here without her.'

His voice gave up on him and he lapsed into silence. Evie could still hear the disturbance in the road outside and wondered if it had been fair to ask Carlos to deal with it.

'I had better go,' he said, pulling himself together. 'If you need me you can contact me at any time. You have my number.'

Evie had feared Eduardo might descend on them and create more friction but apart from one brief telephone call to Felipe to express his condolences he had stayed away.

The temporary housekeeper Felipe had employed was a model of discretion and had made sure the castelo shutters were closed to keep out prying eyes.

With Felipe coming and going at all hours Evie had welcomed her tactful presence in the castelo as she had not relished the idea of being alone in a house that had lost its light and laughter.

'Stay,' Lesli urged when Evie had voiced her indecision, 'if that's what Felipe wants. You've earned his trust — don't throw it away. Apart from anything else, you haven't fulfilled your contract. I presume that gig is still on?'

'I've no idea,' Evie admitted.

'Then use that as your reason to stay. You can say I'm cracking the whip.'

'Olivia and I had almost finished up. There's not a lot more to do.'

'Felipe doesn't know that, does he?'

Evie had to admit he didn't.

'There you are, then.' Lesli paused. 'How are you holding up?' she then asked, showing uncharacteristic concern.

'Astra had such presence,' Evie admitted. 'The castelo isn't the same without her.'

'It's manic over here,' Lesli admitted. 'You've never seen anything like it. I've respected client confidentiality so word has not got out about Astra's catalogue but if Felipe still wants to go ahead with the auction, interest has increased tenfold. Keep me posted.'

In accordance with Astra's wishes, her funeral was to be a private affair. Out of respect the reporters and photographers had stayed away from the small interdenominational chapel and as the cortège wound its way up the hill Evie clasped her bunch of sea pinks to her chest.

The colour complemented Astra's purple mini dress — the one Evie had chosen to wear for the funeral. In accordance with another of Astra's requests, no-one was to wear black, although Evie had draped Astra's black and white checked plaid coat around her shoulders to ward off an unexpected chill in the air.

Below them in the harbour, all activity had ceased for the day. The fishing boats lay idle and there was none of the accustomed bustle in the market place. The stillness of the early afternoon was broken by the gentle hum of bees as they darted in and out the lavender bushes.

An orange butterfly landed briefly on Evie's bouquet, flapped its wings for a second then flew off into the sky.

The service had been simple, discreet and dignified. It was cool inside the chapel with the stained-glass windows reflecting the sun on the polished pews, the ends of which were decorated with Astra's favourite flowers picked from her garden that morning before the blooms had the chance to wilt in the midday sun.

Felipe had paid tribute to his grandmother in a short eulogy that made little reference to her past but featured more on how she had loved her garden and the parties she used to give every summer in aid of the local children's charity.

As they left the chapel a group of children wearing traditional dress sang a tribute fado accompanied by the gentle strains of a guitarra. With eyes lowered they curtseyed to Evie as she and Felipe made their way together back to the castelo.

'Olivia or Catherine should be your escort,' Evie had murmured in Felipe's ear but he had held fast on to her hand and appeared not to hear what she had said.

They entered the garden via the rear footpath to where cool drinks and refreshments had been laid out on the terrace. Serving staff circulated offering trays of canapés to the guests while the local hotelier organised drinks.

'It doesn't seem right to hold a funeral on such a beautiful day,' Olivia looking elegant and chic in an oatmeal shift dress, approached Evie, 'although I think Astra would have approved, don't you?'

'I think she would,' Evie agreed.

'I wasn't sure you'd be here,' Olivia said.

'Felipe asked me to stay on. I hope you don't think I gatecrashed.' Evie's discomfort increased as Olivia subjected her to a searching look.

'I don't think anything of the sort,' she insisted, 'although I'm not sure other people would see it the same way.'

'You mean Catherine?' Evie glanced across to where Olivia's mother was seated, talking to Carlos.

It was the first time Evie had seen her since she had been signed off work.

'I was actually thinking of Eduardo,' Olivia replied.

Mention of his name caused a shiver of apprehension to creep up Evie's spine. Surely he wouldn't carry through his threat to expose her now?

'I was surprised he did not attend the service,' Olivia admitted.

'Do you know where he is?' Evie asked.

'I have no idea.'

Olivia looked over her shoulder and stifled a gasp.

'What's the matter?'

'I spoke too soon,' Olivia said.

Eduardo was standing by the garden gate, his eyes fixed on the pair of them, an unpleasant smile on his face.

The sun chose that moment to disappear behind a cloud, casting a darkened shadow across the garden. Evie shivered as Eduardo walked slowly towards her.

Anger in His Eyes

'So you're still here,' Eduardo sneered at Evie.

'Felipe asked me to stay on.' Evie stood her ground.

'Excuse me, I have to see to my mother.' Olivia cast Evie a sympathetic look then melted away.

'You mean you talked him into it. Did he cry on your shoulder?'

Evie's stomach churned. Neither she nor Felipe had referred to the incident again. How could Eduardo have known? It had to be a lucky guess.

'Hoping to be Mrs Periera, are you?' he persisted. 'I underestimated you. You're smarter than I thought.'

'That's an outrageous thing to say.' Evie could feel her anger mounting but Eduardo remained unperturbed by her outburst.

'You've been raiding Astra's dressing-up

box again I see.' He gestured towards the purple mini dress Evie was wearing.

She tilted her chin at him.

'And I borrowed her plaid coat — with Felipe's permission,' Evie added with heavy emphasis.

'Well, make the most of it. I can afford to wait but not for much longer.' Eduardo re-adopted a threatening tone. 'My patience is wearing thin.'

'I think you'd better leave.' Evie clenched her fists to stop her hands from shaking.

'And I think I'd better stay.' Eduardo beckoned to a hovering waiter and helped himself to a glass of sparkling wine. 'And enjoy the celebration of Astra's life.' He toasted Evie then glanced appreciatively around the garden. 'Soon all this will be mine.'

'Eduardo,' Evie implored through gritted teeth, hoping to appeal to his better nature, 'now is not the time for this conversation.'

She could see Felipe glancing their way and hoped Eduardo wasn't going to make a scene.

'When exactly do you think would be a convenient time for me to tell Felipe all about you and how your family bankrupted the Vicentes?'

Evie now clutched a convenient chair back for support.

'That's not true.' She denied the accusation but nothing she said seemed to faze Eduardo.

'Isn't it?' He shrugged. 'It doesn't matter to me but Felipe may see things differently. He's old-fashioned and proud and things like family honour matter to him.'

'I haven't dishonoured anyone.'

'You can deny everything as much as you like but I know the truth. Your father's behaviour caused Mauricio to have a breakdown. His health was always delicate and he never really recovered.'

Evie felt the ground sway beneath her feet. Her knuckles turned white as she clung on to her garden chair. Eduardo inspected the time on his expensive wristwatch then wrinkled his nose in distaste at the guests.

'Who invited all these village people?'

'They were Astra's friends.' Evie's mouth was so dry she found it difficult to speak.

'That figures. For all her fine airs she was only the daughter of a coal miner and a shop assistant.'

Evie straightened up and let go of her chair. Her father had always taught her to be proud of her roots and Eduardo's intimidation had gone far enough.

'As you are obviously out of your class,' Evie said slowly and clearly, 'perhaps you'd better leave.'

She knew it was an ugly thing to say but it was what Eduardo deserved. His colour deepened and the expression on his face told Evie her barb had hit home.

'You know I really think Felipe should be warned that he has been harbouring a viper.' Eduardo's voice was an angry hiss. 'I wonder if he'll still feel the same about you when he knows the truth?'

'Do as you wish.' Evie tossed her head. 'I'll be going home in the next few days so it doesn't matter what you say about me.'

'Eduardo.' Carlos approached them. 'What is all this?'

'I was having a private word with Evie.'

'I overheard some of it and I have to say your allegations are outrageous. Evie has every right to be here.'

'You would side with her, wouldn't you? You're another one who has fallen for her charms.'

'What on earth do you mean?'

'Early morning jogs? Intimate suppers?'

'There's nothing wrong in that.'

'I've seen how things are between you, but you're wasting your time. Our Evie's got her eye on the big prize. Felipe?' he added as Carlos frowned in disgust.

Felipe detached himself from a local dignitary and approached the group.

'What's going on?' he demanded.

'I'm here to stake my claim,' Eduardo announced. 'Astra only had a lifetime interest in the castelo.'

'I am aware of that.' Felipe towered over the flush-faced Eduardo.

'Good. Then as soon as all the fuss has died down I'll be over to help you move out. Shall we say in a week's time?'

'Not so fast,' Carlos cautioned.

'Stay out of this,' Eduardo snapped. 'This is a family matter.'

'I will not be silenced,' Carlos insisted.

Feeling uncomfortable at the sound of raised voices some of the guests began making their departure.

'Catherine is feeling tired,' Olivia explained. 'One of the charity workers has offered us a lift in her car.' She cast Carlos a curious glance. 'I'll be going back to Faro soon.'

'I should. There's no point in hanging around here — that's if you've got your eye on Carlos,' Edward sneered.

Olivia flushed.

'You'd better fall in with your mother's plans and switch your allegiance to Felipe.

Evie has her eye on Carlos if things with Felipe don't work out. You, my dear Olivia, don't stand a chance.'

'That's not true.'

Evie's attempt to defend herself fell on stony silence until Catherine, who was standing beside her daughter, spoke in rapid Portuguese, all the while casting hostile glances in Evie's direction.

'You see.' Eduardo's smile did not reach his eyes. 'Catherine agrees with me.'

'It's not true, is it?' Olivia asked Evie in a puzzled voice.

'I didn't catch all your mother said,' Evie replied in a shaky voice, 'but I am not here to make trouble.'

Eduardo gave a snort of disgust.

'Go back to Faro, Olivia, and find yourself a real man.'

Carlos moved forward but Felipe restrained him.

'I hope you will excuse us.' Olivia placed a protective arm around Catherine's shoulder. 'My mother is very tired.'

'Of course,' Felipe replied. 'Thank

you for coming.' He bowed towards the older woman. 'Thank you, Catherine, for all you did for my grandmother.'

Catherine, leaning on her daughter's arm, began making slow progress towards the side gate.

'I think you had better explain yourself, Eduardo.' Felipe spoke in a calm voice after Olivia and Catherine had departed. 'You don't need me to tell you your behaviour is bordering on the insulting.'

Soon the garden was empty, save for the small group standing by the terrace. Averting their eyes, the serving staff started to clear away the debris.

'Could you leave that until another time?' Felipe asked the senior waiter.

'We can return later.' He signalled to his staff. 'For the moment we will leave you in peace. Our condolences,' he added in a quiet voice. 'Your grandmother was much respected in the local community.'

'You were right, you know, Felipe,' Eduardo did no more than cast the waiting staff a passing glance, 'when you said you knew nothing about Astra inviting Evie to the castelo. That's because she wasn't invited. Astra put it down to forgetfulness but we know better, don't we, Evie?'

'I have apologised to Evie for my initial misunderstanding of the situation,' Felipe said before Evie could reply. 'Despite what you say, Evie was invited here at my grandmother's request. Now was there anything else?'

'Nice try, Eduardo,' Carlos interjected, 'but your story doesn't hold a grain of truth.'

'Then try this one.' Eduardo's colour deepened.

The garden grew darker as the clouds now completely obliterated the sun. Evie shivered and picking up Astra's coat from where she had draped it over the back of a chair, placed it around her shoulders. Thunder rumbled in the distance.

'Evie used you, Felipe.'

'I fail to see how.'

'To gain access to Astra's private effects. Like me, she wanted to discredit you.'

'She signed a contract,' Carlos said.

'A piece of paper wasn't going to stop her doing what she came here to do.'

'And what exactly was her purpose in coming here?'

'Maybe she was here with the blessing of her agency or whoever it is she works for in London, but the real reason she is here is nothing to do with catalogues or dresses. She came here to find out why your grandfather ruined her father all those years ago. Once she'd found what she was looking for she was going to sell her story to the highest bidder.'

Evie now felt sick as Felipe turned to her, his eyes puzzled.

'Doesn't the name Quinta ring any bells?' Eduardo persisted. 'Francisco Quinta?' he prompted.

'Francisco Quinta?' Carlos repeated in a hollow voice.

'The troublemaking wine merchant?

You can't have forgotten, Carlos. He was the bane of your father's life. He stirred up no end of trouble.'

'Francisco Quinta was before my time but I remember the case notes.' Carlos frowned. 'There was some sort of action group, wasn't there?'

'Now you're getting it,' Eduardo gloated. 'Felipe, how about you?'

The look in Felipe's eyes had turned to cold anger.

'You are related to Francisco Quinta?' he asked Evie.

'He was my father,' Evie admitted.

As rain bounced off the flagstones, she gathered Astra's coat around her shoulders. There was no point in denying the accusation.

'And he was the leader of the action group against my grandfather?' Felipe spoke in a voice Evie barely recognised.

'I don't know,' she replied. 'You'd best discuss it with Eduardo. He seems to have all the facts.'

Evie studied the expression on Felipe's face, waiting for him to say something. The silence lengthened uncomfortably until Evie realised it was clear that he was not going to speak up in her defence.

'If you'll excuse me,' she drew on what remained of her dignity, 'I have a plane to catch.'

End of a Dream?

Evie did not see Felipe again before she left. Throwing her things into her suitcase she called for a taxi then, careful to leave her notes and paperwork regarding Astra's catalogue on the table in the hall, she left for the airport, all within the space of an hour.

If she had hoped that Felipe would come chasing after her to the airport as she had seen happen in countless films then she would be disappointed.

Her flight left on time and a little over three hours later Lesli was waiting for her in the airport arrivals hall ready to scoop her up like a mother hen.

'It's absolutely outrageous.' She grabbed Evie's suitcase and wheeled it through the car park with a determined air. 'Treating you like a common criminal. Felipe Periera hasn't heard the last of this.'

The rear lights of her car flashed

vivid orange in the fading evening light as she flicked her remote control. She swung Evie's case into the boot.

'But first things first. Let's get you home. You're staying with me.' Evie tried to protest but Lesli was having none of it.

'Call it a debriefing session if you like but it's not up for debate. In you get.'

Lesli turned up the heating as she put her foot down on the accelerator, her car eating up the motorway miles as they headed towards London.

'You look chilled to the bone,' she said. 'That dress barely covers your essentials.'

It was then Evie realised she was still wearing Astra's mini dress and clutching her plaid coat.

'It belongs to Astra.' Her voice came out as a half sob. 'So does the coat. Felipe will think I've stolen them.'

'Over my dead body,' Lesli swung into the slower moving late rush hour traffic as she changed lanes. 'Get some rest while I drive us the rest of the way home. You look exhausted.'

Lesli lived alone in an elegant townhouse on the edge of Richmond Park with stunning views over the river. To Evie it was a home from home and she gave a gentle sigh of pleasure as Lesli drew up outside.

'That's more like it.' Lesli gave a nod of approval inspecting Evie's tired face. 'You've got some colour back in your cheeks. Let's get you inside. Mrs Dean's left us soup for supper, with home-baked bread rolls. When did you last eat?'

'I don't remember,' Evie admitted.

'Thought not. What have they been doing to you out there?' She turned her key in the front door. 'No,' she corrected herself, 'we're not going to talk about it now. I prescribe a light supper, a warm bath then an early night. As my dear mother used to say, it'll all seem better in the morning.'

★   ★   ★

Evie awoke to the sound of birds singing through her open window. She snuggled down under her duvet, reluctant to face the world as she recalled the previous day's events. There was a gentle knock on the door.

'Good morning, miss.'

Mrs Dean appeared in the doorway with a tray of tea, toast and orange juice and a single red rose in a white stem vase.

'Ms Scott says you're not to think of getting up until you've eaten and drunk everything on the tray.' She drew back the curtains to let in the sunshine then straightened Evie's pillows. 'There, that's better.' She fussed around the bedroom, picking up Evie's discarded clothes and tidying the dressing table. 'If you want anything just ring the bell. Ms Scott's in the conservatory.'

Evie swung her legs out of the bed and stretched. Lesli was a hard taskmaster but she had a heart of gold and was exactly the right person to have on your side when you were in a jam.

Evie didn't know how she was going to explain all that had happened at the castelo. She hoped it wouldn't overstretch her relationship with her employer.

Lesli looked up from a pile of paperwork as Evie hovered in the doorway.

'Coffee?' She held up the pot.

'I've only just finished breakfast.'

Lesli poured out two mugs of fragrant coffee.

'That's if you change your mind,' she nudged one towards Evie. 'Now start from the beginning.'

Evie picked up one of the mugs, more for something to do with her hands than her need for coffee.

'Eduardo Vicente . . . ' she began and briefly related what had happened.

'I think we should take things further,' Lesli said when Evie finished recounting her story.

'No,' Evie insisted.

'Are you saying no-one knew officially what Astra was up to?'

'Felipe accepted my story — in the end, so did Carlos.'

'That's the legal eagle?' Lesli scratched her head.

'To be honest, at first I thought the commission was a hoax. Some of my models aren't above playing a joke on me and it was April the first but when the electronic payment arrived I knew I had to take things a bit more seriously.

'I suppose I should have double checked but it was a busy day.' Lesli frowned thoughtfully. 'Not a mistake I shall make again in a hurry. From now on everything is double, treble checked.'

'I'm sorry I deceived you,' Evie said, managing to get a word in edgewise.

'What are you talking about now?' Lesli frowned.

'I should have told you about my father.'

'Yes, you should,' Lesli agreed, 'but what's done is done. I've never been one to look back. The decision to send you out to Portugal was mine and I accept full responsibility for what happened. With your knowledge of Portuguese I thought you'd be the ideal choice for the commission.' Lesli paused. 'Did you finish the job, by the way?'

'More or less,' Evie admitted. 'I had help from Olivia Emmanuel.'

'The family retainer's daughter?'

'Yes.'

'And you left the paperwork behind?'

'Everything, apart from the dress I travelled home in, and the coat.'

Lesli made a steeple with her fingers, temporarily lost in thought.

'What are we going to do?' Evie asked.

'For the moment, nothing. As I understand it there is no paper trail connecting us to Felipe Periera and Astra Dempsey's affairs could take an age to sort out so he will be unable to trace us.'

'What about the bank transfer?'

'That will show a payment was made but it could be a time-consuming business to track us down and I should imagine everyone will have more important things on their mind than coming after us.

'We were paid in advance for a job we have completed. Felipe would have no motivation to seek us out.'

'If he should contact you,' Evie said slowly, 'you won't tell him where I am, will you?'

'Guide's honour,' Lesli said, 'but what I do need you to do is to write up a full report of all that happened while it's still fresh in your mind.'

'And Astra's dress and coat?'

'Mrs Dean will see to the dress. The coat will need specialist cleaning so why don't you hang on to both for the moment and we'll see what happens?'

'Shouldn't they be part of the auction?'

'We don't know yet if it's going ahead. Let's lie low and allow things to settle.'

'Thank you, Lesli.'

'What for?'

'Being so understanding.'

'What I don't understand is why you had to go and fall in love with Felipe Periera — wretched man.'

'I am not in love with Felipe Periera.'

Lesli raised a plucked eyebrow.

'Then why didn't you tell him exactly what you thought of him and his family?'

'For heaven's sake, Lesli, it was the day of his grandmother's funeral.'

'I appreciate that, but you didn't have to run away like some Edwardian heroine.'

Evie looked down at the patterned carpet. Until that moment she hadn't been totally sure of her feelings for Felipe but as usual Lesli was right. Evie hadn't wanted to stay on at the castelo to hear Felipe rip her to shreds in front of Carlos and a gloating Eduardo.

'I don't think he feels the same way about me,' Evie admitted, trying not to dwell on the night she and Felipe had shared supper on the terrace and he had presented her with Carlos's crushed rose.

'Then like most men he's a fool.'

'Lesli!' Evie protested.

'Sorry, you're right. There are one or

two exceptions. My own dear Ted, for a start, but look at that Duncan person who ditched you.'

'Let's not go there, Lesli,' Evie pleaded.

'Mind you,' Lesli took no notice of Evie's interruption, 'I'm not blaming you for falling for your handsome Portuguese. Felipe Periera would catch any girl's eye. Right, we'd better get on,' she added briskly.

Evie spent the rest of the day writing her report for Lesli. It ran to several pages and until then she hadn't realised quite how much of an impact the episode had made on her life.

Her report conjured up memories of the fishermen in the harbour unloading their catch. It evoked the smell of the flowers in Astra's beloved garden. Evie could hear laughter and the tinkle of teacups on the terrace. It had been a dream time but like all dreams it had come to an end.

'Finished yet?' Lesli poked her head round the door at the end of the day.

'I need to go through it one last time,' Evie turned off her screen, 'but I think I'm there.'

'Then come on through, there's something I want you to see. You can finish up in the morning.'

Evie followed Lesli through to her drawing-room.

'I recorded this earlier for you.' She turned on the television. A picture of a young Astra filled the screen. 'The camera loved her, didn't it?'

Evie agreed as she looked at the gallery of photos.

'Interest is beginning to die down but there's still a lot of speculation doing the rounds.'

'About what?'

'The old story about why she disappeared and the reason for it. I suppose we'll never know now. One last thing . . . I did find out about Shaun Merrony — you remember, the famous photographer?'

'What about him?'

'Apparently his mother is still alive.

She's never really got over her son's death. He was her only child and the reporter who tracked her down said her one real regret was that she never met Astra as she feels sure she would have made her son a wonderful wife and been a good mother to his children.'

'What a strange thing to say.'

'Isn't it?'

'Anyway, why don't you take a couple of days off and chill out? You can stay on here for as long as you like. I have to fly off to Milan early in the morning, so you'd be doing me a favour by house sitting. You can check the mail and if you think there's anything of importance call me and don't forget to water the plants.'

*   *   *

The next afternoon, Evie went for a long walk through the park. The daffodils were past their best and their drooping heads were a sad reminder that Easter was over.

She watched several children play an energetic game of hide and seek as dog walkers strolled by, glad to be out in the fresh air.

She sat down on a bench, her head still in a whirl. Lesli had been generous and sympathetic but Evie still couldn't help feeling she had let everyone down.

Personal life should never be allowed to intrude into professional life and she had broken that rule in a spectacular fashion.

It was then Evie realised her mobile was vibrating in her pocket.

'Darling!' It was her mother's voice. 'How are you? It's been ages since we heard from you and your father and I were beginning to get a bit worried. What have you been up to?'

A Message from Portugal

'Goodness, there's a name from the past!' Clare Quinta laughed down the line. 'I haven't thought about the Vicente family for years. Of course, your father was very upset — we both were — but he's moved on and he no longer holds a grudge against the Vicentes, but at the time it was a different story.'

'You never did tell me what happened.'

'Why do you want to know now?'

'The family have been in the news because of Astra Dempsey.'

'She was that model, wasn't she? The one in the famous photograph?'

'She also married Mauricio Vicente.'

'Your father liked Mauricio and I remember his wife had a lovely garden. That side of the family were good to us. I caught occasional glimpses of Astra but I never really knew her and my time was taken up looking after you and the vineyard. They were busy days.

'It was Mauricio's brother Antonio who stirred things up. He was the reckless one, always in trouble of some sort. Poor Mauricio got the blame for the family losses but it wasn't his fault. Antonio wasn't popular in the village. He never paid any bills and was regularly involved in money-making schemes that never worked out.

'Eventually local goodwill and his credit ran out. Land had to be sold off to pay the mounting debts.

'Although the vineyard was a going concern it was reclaimed. As a result we were homeless and penniless. We didn't own the vineyard so there was nothing we could do.'

'Did Papa take the family to court?'

'He thought about it and sought legal advice. Letters were exchanged but at the end of the day he decided it wasn't worth it. There was a notary in the village, a man called Sébastien Diego, who gave your father some valuable advice.

'He said we would only lose the small amount of money we had left if we pursued our claim.

'Although it broke your father's heart at the time, he came to realise it was probably for the best but there were some ugly scenes.

'The community protest group was very active. Your father was chairman and in revenge Antonio tried to blame your father for the vineyard's demise but that just wasn't true. The vineyard was a thriving business. Our order books were full and we were working to capacity.'

'So Papa didn't bankrupt the family?'

'They did that to themselves.'

Evie paused. Her mother hadn't mentioned Mauricio's breakdown. Had this perhaps been another of Eduardo's fabrications?

'Anyway, it's all in the past and not worth talking about. When are you coming over to visit us?'

'As soon as I can,' Evie promised.

'Make sure you do. I am in desperate need of some girl talk with my daughter.'

'Give my love to Papa.'

Evie stood up. Her mother's call had taken a great weight off her mind and for the first time since she had flown home she felt like smiling.

There was a spring in her step as she made her way back to Lesli's house to finish her report while the details were still fresh in her mind.

Determinedly not thinking about Felipe Periera or the way his dark brown eyes would soften into a smile when something amused him or the tenderness of his voice when he was talking to his grandmother, she tried to remain as factual as possible.

She decided to omit any reference to Astra's dress and coat currently hanging in her wardrobe. It would be difficult to return them to the castelo anonymously and the last thing she wanted was Felipe discovering her whereabouts and descending on her threatening to sue for the unauthorised removal of family property.

Evie felt sorry that she had not been able to say a proper goodbye to Olivia or Carlos. From what Evie's mother had said, Carlos's father Sébastien had been good to her own father and she would have liked to express her gratitude to Carlos.

A few days later the e-mail landed in her inbox. Feeling she couldn't rely indefinitely on Lesli's hospitality Evie had moved back into her bedsit and after a day's intensive paperwork catching up on her backlog her head was spinning.

Lesli was involved in another high-profile project and back to her usual snappy self. She had allowed Evie to go home after work that evening only on the promise that she would remain online should anything important come through regarding the latest contract.

It was not unknown for Lesli to want her to work through until midnight.

Evie scrolled through her e-mails

deleting her spam messages before the name Olivia Emmanuel leaped out at her. She sat back with a gasp of surprise before eventually deciding to open it.

'Hi, Evie,' she read, 'I managed to track you down through Carlos. He's very discreet so please don't blame him. I had an appointment with him in his office. He was called away. Your file was open on the desk. That contract thing you signed was on top and I caught sight of your e-mail address.'

Evie bit her lip. She remembered now. Carlos had pencilled it in after she'd signed it. She prayed Felipe wouldn't be as resourceful as Olivia in tracking her down.

'I did ask before I pinched it,' Olivia's e-mail continued. 'Anyway, I am sorry you had to leave so suddenly. Everyone's being very tight-lipped about what happened but I can guess.

'My mother has been unwell and my time has been taken up looking after her so I haven't caught up on the latest gossip.

'What I can tell you is that my mother will not be returning to the castelo. Felipe has arranged for her to receive a pension and she has decided to move in with her sister who lives outside Faro.

'The castelo has been closed up. Eduardo has been making a nuisance of himself and being most unpleasant to everyone. Carlos gave me the barest details about the incident in the garden after we left.

'I do not understand Eduardo's accusation but I want you to know I do not believe you are a spy (despite my mother's accusations).' Here Olivia had inserted a smiley emoticon.

'My mother wants me to say sorry to you. She now realises how rude she was and can only put her behaviour down to the fact she was not feeling well.' There followed more emoticons.

'We now come to the important part of this e-mail. Carlos told me Felipe has decided to go ahead with the auction. Should Eduardo inherit the castelo then Astra's effects will need to be taken care of. Felipe has no need of them and he realises he could raise a lot of money for Astra's charity if her fashion collection were put up for sale.

'I will let you know the details when I have them. I think we should be top of the invitation list. After all, we put in a lot of work, didn't we?

'Please keep in touch. I miss you and would love to catch up again some day.

'By the way, Carlos sends his love. We have been in communication a lot over my mother and the business of the auction and, well, we shall see how things go between us. Lots of love, Olivia.'

Evie re-read the e-mail several times. She was glad Olivia and Carlos were more than just good friends and that Catherine appeared to have removed her objection to their relationship. She was glad too that the older woman was now her friend.

She wondered briefly where Felipe was now. His work took him all over the world but with so much to do regarding

Astra's estate it might be difficult for him to travel away from Europe.

'So they're going ahead with it?' Lesli greeted the news with the raise of an eyebrow. 'I can't say I'm surprised. What would Felipe Periera want with an attic full of his grandmother's old clothes?'

'They're hardly that,' Evie objected.

'You're right.' Lesli slapped her desk with the open palm of her hand. 'This should stir up a media storm. I wonder if there is going to be a private viewing beforehand? Everyone will be fighting like cats and dogs to get an invitation.'

'What do we do about the dress and coat?' Evie asked. 'They're still in your wardrobe.'

'Let me put out a few feelers and find out the latest gossip,' Lesli said, ignoring her question. 'Will you go?'

'Where?' Evie asked with a frown.

'To the auction, of course.'

'Surely it will be by invitation only.'

'And surely you'll be on the list. Didn't your friend Olivia say so?'

'I hope Felipe won't know how to contact me.'

'Maybe you could go as Olivia's guest?'

'I don't think so.'

'Why ever not?'

'Isn't it obvious?'

'You've nothing to be ashamed of. Face up to your demons, I say.'

'I don't have any.'

'Then what's your objection to going to the auction?'

'I don't have to give a reason.'

'This is about Felipe Periera, isn't it?'

'Of course it isn't.'

'I don't believe you.'

'It's just I didn't expect to like Astra Dempsey quite so much,' Evie confessed. 'I wasn't on a revenge trip despite what everyone thinks but when I flew out to Portugal I did want to put my mind at rest over my father's past. No-one would ever talk about it.

'Then Felipe fulfilled my pre-conceived ideas of how arrogant the male members of the Vicente family could be. It was only later that I had cause to revise my opinion.'

'Perhaps Felipe revised his opinion about you.'

'If Felipe Periera gives me a moment's thought,' Evie insisted, 'it is as the daughter of the man who ruined his family.'

'That is absolute tosh. From what you tell me your friend Olivia doesn't believe it and I shouldn't expect Carlos does, either, and whatever you say about Felipe he's nobody's fool. I tell you what he is though — he's a red-blooded male and you're a beautiful girl, a real diamond.'

Evie's cheeks flamed. She wasn't used to being referred to as beautiful or a diamond and compliments did not usually flow from Lesli's lips.

'Felipe would be mad not to fall in love with you and if he didn't then you're right. Maybe there is no room in your life for him, but,' a mischievous look crossed Lesli's face, 'if I were you, I'd keep the door open.

'Go to the auction and if you really

don't see yourself as Felipe's soulmate you can always tell him what you think of his behaviour . . . All right, I'm coming,' Lesli bellowed into her intercom as it buzzed loudly on the desk.

A week later Evie received an e-mail from Carlos telling her the auction was scheduled for the following week. A personal invitation was attached.

Declaration of Love

'The word on the street is it's going to be huge,' Lesli informed Evie.

It was late evening and they were sitting in her office going over the events of the day. This was the first chance Evie had had to talk at length to Lesli and although they didn't normally drink in the office Lesli had bought a bottle of wine to celebrate the conclusion of another successful contract.

The sun cast a setting glow on the trees in the park outside the window and Evie's thoughts strayed to the magnificent sunsets at the castelo when it seemed as if the sky had set fire to the horizon.

'Are you listening to me?' Lesli demanded.

'Sorry.' Evie returned her attention to Lesli. 'You were talking about the auction?'

'Hmm.' Lesli cast her a speculative glance.

When Evie had insisted on sticking by her decision not to attend, she and Lesli had experienced one of their frankest ever exchanges of views.

'Are you serious?'

'Never more so.'

'What has got into you?' Lesli demanded.

'Nothing. I don't want to go, that's all.'

'I wouldn't have thought you were the type to hold a grudge or sulk.'

'That's silly talk.'

'Is it?'

'Yes,' Evie insisted.

'Felipe Periera is not going to clap you in irons, you know,' Lesli said.

'Maybe not but has it escaped your memory that we do still have two valuable articles of clothing belonging to Astra hanging in your wardrobe?'

'Then wouldn't the auction be a good opportunity to speak to Felipe and explain the situation and put all the other stuff right between you at the same time?

'I mean, he can hardly start hurling

accusations at you in a crowded auction room, can he?'

'He'll be too busy to talk to me.'

'Then what's the problem?'

Evie paused to think things through before realising Lesli did present a valid case. The auction would probably be the last chance she would have to see Felipe. Maybe she did need to clear the air and if she couldn't speak to him she could leave a note.

'So, will you rethink your decision?' In the face of Evie's hesitation, Lesli pushed home her advantage.

With a reluctant nod of her head and a sigh Evie had indicated that she would.

'Good, that's settled. Now no more mooning about the place with a face like a wet weekend. You are to put on your glad rags, hold your head up high and don't take any nonsense from anyone, otherwise they'll have me on their case.'

Lesli's eyes lit up as she inspected the gold invitation.

'Hey, there's even a special entrance for VIPs. I know people who would kill for one of these. Security is going to be tight. What are you going to wear?'

'I hadn't given it any thought,' Evie admitted.

'Wait here.'

Lesli was back moments later with a selection of outfits.

'Try this.' She held out a deep blue velvet dress, with three-quarter sleeves and a draping cowl neckline. 'I've some earrings to match somewhere and a contemporary look is called for, I think. What about a sequin embroidered denim jacket?'

Knowing it was futile to argue with Lesli, Evie tried the dress on and stood in front of the office mirror. The colour brought out the amber flecks in her blue eyes. Evie had to hand it to Lesli. She knew her stuff.

'You need to wear good underwear. Velvet takes no prisoners,' Lesli insisted, 'and black tights to showcase your legs. I'll leave that side of things to you. Now

I'm relying on you to knock 'em dead.'

Evie put a hand on Lesli's shoulder and leaning forward kissed her cheek.

'Stop that.' Lesli stepped back, but Evie could tell by the expression on her face she was touched by the gesture.

'If I didn't have you as a friend I'd have to invent you,' Evie said.

'I haven't a clue what you're talking about but I haven't gone to all this trouble to have you mess up at the last moment.'

'I won't,' Evie had promised, but the next morning, standing on the pavement outside the prestigious gallery hosting the auction, Evie was having serious second thoughts.

The smart set were out in force and she recognised several high-profile names in the fashion industry strutting down the red carpet smiling for the cameras with practised ease before submitting to the strict security in the private roped off area.

Feeling out of place but remembering Lesli's lecture, Evie skirted the red carpet and made her way to the VIP entrance via the pavement. A uniformed security guard stepped forward just as Evie was shouldered aside.

'I don't need an invitation, I'm family,' the new arrival addressed the security guard.

'I'm sorry, sir,' the guard explained. 'No-one is to be admitted without an invitation.'

Evie shrank into the shadows.

'That rule doesn't apply to me.'

'It applies to everyone, sir.'

'This is outrageous. Astra Dempsey was married to my uncle.'

'May I have your name please, sir?'

'Eduardo Vicente.'

'I'm afraid there is no-one of that name on the list.'

'Who is your superior officer?'

Another man stepped forward.

'May I be of assistance, sir?'

Eduardo was escorted to a quieter area and with his attention diverted Evie seized her chance and stepping forward produced her invitation.

'Thank you, Ms Quinta.' The guard checked her name off the list. 'If you'll just put your handbag on the belt and take off your jacket you can go through security.'

Evie helped herself to an orange juice from the tray of drinks offered. She refused the champagne, knowing she needed to keep a clear head. One or two of the guests acknowledged her with pleasant smiles but she didn't recognise anyone and lacked the courage to break into a group.

Putting down her drink she glanced through the catalogue and immediately recognised several of the photos and descriptions. Absorbed in her copy of the catalogue, Evie didn't notice a well-dressed elderly woman approaching.

'I think you're like me.' She spoke with an American accent, 'you don't appear to know anybody here either, Ms . . . ?'

'Evie Quinta.'

The woman shook her hand.

'I have to say I absolutely love your

jacket. Time was when I could wear sequins, but not any more. When you get to my age it looks vulgar. I'm Nancy Merrony.'

'Shaun Merrony's mother?' Evie blinked in surprise.

'You've heard of my son?'

'Who hasn't?' Evie replied.

'Do you think,' Mrs Merrony touched her elbow, 'we could sit down?' She indicated her stick. 'I find I can't stand for a long time these days.'

'Of course.'

Evie led her over to one of the velvet-backed chairs.

'Thank you. I don't often attend these events and I can't remember the last time I flew across the Atlantic but I couldn't miss this occasion. My husband passed away many years ago and these days I live a quiet life, but there was a time when we partied every day.'

'He was a diplomat, wasn't he?'

'He was indeed. We travelled the world but he liked his London posting the best. He always said it was because

210

he didn't have to struggle to make himself understood as everyone spoke our language.' She laughed.

'I had to remind him that English was actually your language, not ours.' Mrs Merrony gave a happy sigh. 'It's good to be back, even though everything has changed so much. Knowing of my interest in the collection the ambassador's wife invited me. Wasn't that kind of her?'

'Very,' Evie agreed looking around the room.

There was no sign of Eduardo or Felipe.

'Tell me, what is your connection with Astra Dempsey?' Mrs Merrony asked.

Evie had decided if anyone asked that question she would keep her reply simple and truthful.

'I helped compile the catalogue,' she explained.

'Did you indeed? That must have been fascinating.'

'Did you know Astra?' Evie asked.

A look of sadness crossed Mrs Merrony's face.

'No, I never met her and that's something I really regret. Tell me, Miss Quinta . . . '

'Evie, please.'

'Evie, then, and you must call me Nancy. Have you ever done something you wish you hadn't?'

'On occasions,' Evie admitted.

'I'm not proud of my behaviour many years ago.' Nancy seemed lost in thought, 'It took the loss of the woman I once disliked more than anyone on this earth to realise I was so very wrong.'

A disturbance drew their attention to the doorway. Evie swallowed the nervous lump of apprehension clogging her throat.

'Who is that?' Nancy Merrony asked.

'Felipe Periera, Astra's grandson.'

'Darling,' Nancy held tight on to Evie's hand, 'help me to my feet. You absolutely have to introduce me.'

All eyes swivelled in their direction as

Felipe spotted them and strode towards them. He was wearing a business suit and the crisp white of his shirt highlighted his open-air tan. His hair was swept back in a style that suggested he had attended to it in a hurry. Beside her Evie heard Nancy give a little gasp.

'Is it really you?' she asked in a frail voice.

'I don't believe I've had the pleasure.' Felipe addressed Nancy with a courteous bow.

'I don't believe you have,' she replied, seemingly recovering her composure. 'I'm Nancy Merrony. Your grandmother and my son were,' she paused, 'great friends.'

'It's a pleasure to meet you.'

'You don't know how pleased I am to meet you, too.' Nancy raised a hand then gave an embarrassed half laugh. 'Please don't let me detain you. I'm sure you've more important people to talk to.'

'I can't think of any,' Felipe replied. Nancy smiled affectionately at him.

'Bless you,' she said in a soft voice.

For a moment it was as if Nancy and Felipe were the only two people in the room. Evie wondered if it might be a good moment to slip into the background but before she could move, Nancy touched her arm.

'Do you know my young companion Evie Quinta?' she asked Felipe.

'Yes, I do.'

The look he gave Evie almost had her toppling back into her seat.

'Of course you do. She did an excellent job compiling your catalogue, didn't she?' Nancy looked past Felipe's shoulder. 'And who is this young lady?'

'Hi, everyone.'

'Olivia!' Evie gasped in delight at the sight of her smiling face. 'I didn't know you were coming.'

'I wouldn't have missed it for the world. Everyone's here.'

'Including Eduardo?'

'His name was not on the guest list,' Felipe said.

'I saw him outside,' Evie stuttered.

214

'No-one gets in without an invitation.'

'Young lady,' Nancy took charge of the situation as she addressed Olivia, 'will you please escort me to the buffet? I feel in need of sustenance.'

'What? Oh, yes, of course.' Olivia winked at Evie. 'It's this way.'

'Thank you so much.' Nancy linked her arm through Olivia's. 'I hope to meet you again very soon, Felipe.' She paused. 'You don't mind me using your first name?'

'Of course not.'

'Only I feel I've known you for years.' She raised her hand to his face and stroked it then with careful steps allowed Olivia to lead her towards the buffet.

'We have to talk,' Evie hissed, aware that Felipe's presence was attracting attention.

'There I would agree with you.'

'About the purple mini dress and the checked tweed coat.'

Evie knew she was gabbling but it was difficult to concentrate with Felipe's eyes scorching her skin.

'I didn't mean to travel home wearing them but there wasn't time to change.'

'Shut up.' Felipe's lips barely moved as he spoke.

'I beg your pardon?' Evie faltered.

This was a nightmare. Why on earth had she let Lesli talk her into attending the auction?

'Do you want me to take drastic action to stop you talking nonsense?'

He moved towards her.

'You're invading my body space,' Evie protested.

'That's not all I'll do if you don't tell me why you flew off in a huff without telling anyone where you were going.'

'Eduardo exposed me as a fraud.'

'It's what you are, isn't it?' Evie stared mutely at Felipe. 'A fraud?' he repeated.

'Then you do believe what he said about me?'

'A fraud I happen to have fallen in love with.'

'No,' Evie's denial came out as a low moan. 'You can't say things like that, not here.'

'Where would you like me to say them?'

'You don't understand. My father . . . ' she began.

'Sounds like the sort of man I admire.'

'He made a lot of trouble for your family.'

'He stood up for his rights. What would you have had him do? Roll over and give in?'

'I'm sorry to interrupt.' One of the auctioneers tiptoed towards them.

'What?' Felipe swung round to face him.

'You did say we needed to make a prompt start to the proceedings,' he glanced at the wall clock, 'and it's now ten minutes past schedule.'

The guests were beginning to take their seats and all the telephone booths were occupied for those wishing to make bids from abroad.

'Don't disappear again,' Felipe insisted, 'I need to talk to you.'

Evie watched him cross the floor, greeting casual acquaintances and friends with a smile. A lump caught in her throat. She knew she must never see Felipe Periera again.

The Secret Is Out

Unsure where to go and anxious to avoid the crowds still thronging the pavements outside the auction house, Evie headed for the underground station.

She had to get away from Felipe as fast as she could. She jumped on the first train that rattled into the station then counted the stations down to Richmond to the sanctuary of Lesli's house.

She hurried along the tow-path. On any other day she would have lingered by the water. She always enjoyed watching the activities on the Thames, but today there wasn't time.

Mrs Dean answered the door on the first ring.

'Evie, I wasn't expecting you today, was I?' she greeted her with a friendly smile.

'I need to check something upstairs,' Evie replied, 'but please don't let me get in your way.'

'Will you be staying long? Only I need to do some shopping.'

'I'll let myself out,' Evie assured her, 'and I'll lock up afterwards.'

'In that case I'll leave you to it.'

Evie hovered on the threshold of the bedroom. She wasn't normally fanciful but she had the feeling today was a momentous day.

Lesli would probably go mad when she realised Evie had walked out on the auction but what else could she have done? Felipe had called her a fraud.

She ignored the small voice inside her head telling her he had also said he'd fallen in love with her. He couldn't have been thinking straight. Their lifestyles and past history would tear them apart.

On trembling legs Evie made her way across the room towards the wardrobe, her feet sinking into the deep pile carpet. She unlocked the door.

It creaked open to reveal Astra's dress and coat. Carefully removing them from their hangers, Evie spread them out on the bed.

The situation was impossible. Despite her mother's assurances that her father had moved on Evie was convinced her father would be crushed if she had a relationship with a Vicente.

Like Felipe he was a proud Portuguese and the wounds the Vicente family had inflicted on her father would run deep. Not being Portuguese her mother would not feel the same but Evie had Portuguese blood in her veins. She shared her father's pride.

Felipe Periera had virtually accused her of being a liar and a thief.

He hadn't trusted her from the beginning and that was why he had made her sign a disclaimer saying she wouldn't remove anything from the castelo.

Well, she had and the evidence was lying on the bed in front of her. She had broken the terms of her contract and there was no going back.

She looked round for some tissue paper. Lesli used a reputable courier company to carry out their deliveries. Evie decided she would employ them to send the coat and dress back to Felipe under cover of Lesli's agency.

She picked up the coat and slipping her arms through the sleeves wrapped it around her body, hugging it to her. She felt as though she were saying one last goodbye to Astra.

It was as if the coat understood and hugged her back. Evie could almost hear Astra's laugh and her voice in the background telling Evie life was for living.

She ran her hands down the pockets. The stitching was coming apart in places through years of wear and tear. Wiggling her fingers through the hole she felt something stiff in the lining.

Taking the coat off she ran her hands along the seam. Anxious not to further damage the lining by sticking her hand all the way down the hole she jiggled the envelope back towards the pocket opening. Eventually it slid out of the lining. Evie saw it wasn't an envelope but a sheet of folded paper.

Intrigued, she sat on the bed and debated what to do. The paper was stiff, looked official and smelt musty. It must have been hidden inside the coat lining for a long time.

The trunk had been locked away in the attic for goodness knew how many years. Evie imagined no-one had been up there in ages. Astra had wanted the door on her past closed.

Had she known this document was hidden in her coat or had she misplaced it in her usual scatty fashion then forgotten all about it?

Sensing whatever she was holding might be important Evie debated what to do. Should she mail it to Felipe? What if it went astray? She turned it over, her fingertips gliding over the back of an embossed crest.

Coming to a decision that went against her nature and with trembling fingers Evie unfolded the sheet of paper. As she read the contents her jaw dropped.

Eduardo had been right all along. There was no way Evie could courier the dress and coat back to Felipe now. She had to see him, but had she left it too late? Thrusting the coat and dress back into the wardrobe she raced out of the house and back to the underground station.

Delays on the line caused the journey to take much longer than usual. Frustrated, Evie could only sit and wait while the driver promised they would be on their way as soon as possible.

Guests were drifting away from the auction as Evie approached a security guard.

'I'm sorry, madam,' he apologised, 'I can't let you in without your invitation.'

'But I had one this morning. If you check you'll find my name on the list.'

'It's more than my job's worth to let you in. There was a gentleman here earlier who made a tremendous fuss, said he was a member of the family but he didn't have an official invitation so he wasn't let in.'

'I was here at the same time,' Evie attempted to explain.

'It still doesn't alter anything.'

'Evie?' She heard a voice behind her call out her name.

'Nancy,' Evie greeted the older woman, 'can you help?'

'What's the problem?'

'I have to get in to see Felipe but I've misplaced my invitation.'

'He's gone,' Nancy said.

'Where?'

'Back to Portugal, I think. He was very annoyed to find you'd left before he had a chance to talk to you. Where did you go?'

'It's a long story.'

'Then save it for a more appropriate time. Look, there's my driver. Why don't I give you a lift somewhere?'

Evie shook her head.

'I don't know where I'm going.'

'I do,' Nancy said with a cheerful smile. 'You're going to Portugal and my driver will take you to the airport.'

Evie blinked at Nancy. That smile — she'd seen it so many times.

'Nancy,' she said slowly, 'there's something I ought to tell you but I can't right now.'

'No there isn't,' Nancy said in a soft voice and squeezed her hand. 'I've waited this long I can wait a little longer — but not too long. Tell me your story when you're ready. Now,' the chauffeur drew up beside them and leaped out to open the door, 'get in and we'll get you to the airport and don't you dare walk out on Felipe again.'

So Many Memories

Evie stood outside the castelo and stared in shocked disbelief at the shuttered windows. She peered over the side gate that led to Astra's beloved garden. Weeds were vying for space with the flowers. Already the castelo had the neglected look of an unoccupied property.

'He isn't here.'

Evie spun round.

'Catherine?' Her voice faltered.

'Before you ask, the castelo has been closed up and I don't know where Felipe is. I presume that is why you are here?'

'Do you know when Felipe will be back?' Evie asked.

'I don't,' was the crisp reply. She indicated a convenient wooden bench. Catherine made herself comfortable then looked up at Evie.

'You can tell me all about it if you like,' she coaxed. 'I can be very discreet, I've had enough practice.'

Evie sank down beside Catherine clutching her bag and the few personal possessions she had managed to cram into a holdall before Nancy's chauffeur had driven her to the airport.

From what Nancy had hinted it seemed she was aware of the true nature of the relationship between her son and Astra.

'Don't make the same mistake I did,' Nancy said. 'I've missed out on so much because of my stupid pride. Before my marriage I was a Hartshorn and the Hartshorns did not mix outside their social circle. Can you believe it? What a prig I must have been.

'Darling, I know I don't have the right to lecture you on such a short acquaintance but please take some advice from someone who knows. I've made some big mistakes in my time and if I could turn the clock back I would. Tell Felipe how you feel about him. Tell him you love him.'

'I don't.'

'There you go again, denying the obvious.' Nancy looked angry. 'Please, for my sake? Will you do as I ask?'

Evie hesitated then gave a reluctant nod.

'Good girl. Now get yourself off to the airport and keep in touch.'

'I don't know where to start,' Evie now admitted to Catherine. 'It's complicated.'

'Then let me help you. The Vicentes are a proud family.'

'Like the Hartshorns,' Evie put in.

'Who?' Catherine frowned.

'Never mind. It was just something someone said to me. Go on,' Evie urged.

'It's really your turn now.'

Evie took a deep breath.

'I'm not sure how much you know already.'

'You are referring to Astra's past?'

'Yes.'

Catherine made a gesture with her head.

'I know nothing for sure but shall we say I suspected?'

'What did you suspect?'

'That Cassandra was not Mauricio's daughter. As she grew up I sensed she didn't belong. Mauricio was a good father but Cassandra was a wild child. She would never obey him and it was as if at times he didn't care what she did.

'A true father would have worried more about the company she was keeping. Astra was the one who tried to tame her but she wasn't strict enough with the child.' Catherine looked out towards the sea. 'You know Cassandra ran away and married without her parents' consent?'

'Carlos told me.'

'Then when she died and Astra adopted Felipe I knew for certain.'

'That Mauricio wasn't his natural grandfather?'

'There was no physical likeness and it was the same old story. Mauricio wasn't a harsh man but sometimes he was too strict with Felipe. It was as if he resented the boy's presence.

'Perhaps he felt that Cassandra had let them down and after she ran away he wanted to wash his hands of her. He must have hoped that for the first time in their marriage he would have Astra all to himself, but it wasn't to be.'

'He really loved Astra?'

'More than life itself.'

'And Astra, did she love Mauricio?'

'I always had the feeling there was someone else. She was never unfaithful or anything like that and she settled to life in Marina and was well regarded in the village.

'In her own way I suppose she loved Mauricio but eventually I came to the conclusion that he was not Cassandra's father and as such not the great love of Astra's life.'

'Were you here when Astra married Mauricio?'

'No member of either family attended the service. It was a quiet ceremony. Astra's father had recently died and her mother did not want to travel to Portugal, having never been away from home.

'Raffelo disinherited Mauricio and Antonio was off somewhere with his rich friends. Even if he had been home I don't think he would have been a wedding witness.'

Catherine turned her attention back to Evie.

'How did you discover Cassandra's true parentage?'

'I found her birth certificate.'

Catherine gave a rueful smile.

'I knew you'd be trouble from the moment you arrived.'

'Is that why you didn't want me to go rooting around in the attic?'

'Partly. Astra was growing forgetful and tired and I had a sense that the attic held the secret to her past. No-one was ever allowed up there. Then out of the blue Astra came up with the idea of auctioning her fashion collection. I tried to dissuade her but you know how stubborn she could be.'

'I do,' Evie agreed.

'If she had secreted away her personal papers, I didn't want Eduardo finding them and if we opened up the attic I knew it would only be a matter of time before he began poking his nose into affairs that didn't concern him.

'He had been trying to prove that Astra and Mauricio weren't married for years and that he was the heir to the castelo.'

'He was partly right,' Evie acknowledged, 'but not for the reason he suspected.'

'Astra and Mauricio were married — there was no doubt.'

'But Felipe is not the heir to the castelo.'

They lapsed into silence for several moments before Catherine spoke.

'I hear you are Francisco Quinta's daughter and that Eduardo blackmailed you?'

'He said that unless I could come up with something to his advantage he would tell Felipe all about me.'

'Which is what he did after the funeral service?'

'How did you know?'

'Carlos told Olivia and she told me.'

'Did you know my father?'

'Not well. I felt sorry for what happened to him, but he wasn't the only one affected by the Vicentes' extravagances. Poor Mauricio. He had to bear the brunt of everyone's anger. Antonio made himself scarce and Raffelo put it about that what happened was Mauricio's fault.

'The villagers only started to trust Mauricio again after Astra immersed herself in local charity work. He was an unlucky man. The fates were unkind to him in more ways than one.' Catherine paused. 'Why do you want to see Felipe?' she asked.

'I still have Astra's coat and dress,' Evie explained. 'They should have been included in the auction.'

'Is that the only reason?'

Evie could feel a flush of embarrassment working its way up her neck. First Nancy Merrony, now Catherine Emmanuel. Were her feelings for Felipe so obvious?

'I have to tell him about his mother.'

'He may already know.'

'Then why hasn't Eduardo taken possession of the castelo?'

'I don't know.' Catherine shook her head. 'If you want to you can leave the dress and coat with me. I will make sure Felipe gets them.'

'I can carry them inside for you,' Evie offered.

'I no longer have a key to the castelo. Eduardo was becoming a nuisance and tried to take it from me once or twice so I gave it back to Felipe. I am going to live with my sister in Faro and no longer need it.'

'What will you do with the coat and dress?'

'Hang them in a cupboard. Felipe pays my rent so even if I do not see him again he will find the clothes. I will write him a note and explain.'

'I may not see you again, either.' Evie spoke slowly. 'My time here is over.'

'In that case,' Catherine suggested, 'why don't you take a short walk down to your father's old vineyard to make your goodbyes?'

'Do you think the current owners would mind?'

'Not at all. It's now a restaurant. All the young professionals go there. Why don't you have a glass of wine to toast your father? I won't come with you,' Catherine forestalled Evie's invitation, 'I have too much to do but again I apologise for my earlier behaviour towards you. It was for the best of reasons, I hope you understand.'

Handing over the dress and coat Evie watched Catherine stow them in her bag before getting slowly to her feet.

'Are you sure you wouldn't like me to carry them down the hill for you?' she asked.

'My doctor tells me exercise is important, and as long as I go at my own pace I can manage. Thank you,' she added.

Evie was glad she and Catherine had finally parted as friends. She glanced at her watch. She should really head back to the airport to catch a flight home but she couldn't resist taking Catherine up on her suggestion. She had to have one last chance to look round.

The vineyard had been re-named. Adega meant winery and Evie was pleased the new owners had picked an appropriate name.

Her old home stood by the side of the road, a whitewashed building decorated in the traditional style with brightly coloured tile motifs.

What had been the vineyard itself was now laid out with tables and chairs and several people were sitting around under the sunshades, enjoying the last of the afternoon sunshine.

Evie settled down at one of the wooden tables and picked up the wine menu. Choosing a red that she knew would have earned her father's approval she ate the nuts the waiter had placed in a small bowl in front of her.

Nancy Merrony had said she would be staying on in London for a few days visiting old friends before she flew home. Evie decided her only choice was to leave the copy of Cassandra's birth certificate with her. Nancy could decide what to do with it.

She swirled her wine around in her glass enjoying the deep ruby red colour that signified a good vintage.

Her eyes misted over. There were so many memories here in this garden. She could almost remember taking her first steps and wailing in distress as she fell to her knees on the harsh scorched earth before a firm pair of hands picked her up.

A shadow fell across the table. Shading her eyes she looked up.

'Catherine told me I would find you here,' he said.

Is This Love?

'Do you mind if I join you?'

Felipe signalled to the waiter to bring another glass of wine then, without waiting for Evie's assent, sat down.

The evening sun slanted across the old vineyard turning his hair a deep chestnut. His resemblance to the photo Evie had seen of Shaun Merrony was unmistakeable. Nancy must have noticed it too.

They had the same dark brown eyes, high cheekbones and brooding good looks, but this evening there was none of Felipe's earlier haughty arrogance. He now looked like a man who had discovered a few home truths.

Had Nancy told him he was her great-grandson? If she had then Evie could sympathise with him. She knew how the past could come as a shock.

'It was Nancy's idea,' he said slowly.

'What was?'

'She said I had to get out here fast before you changed your mind.' An angry frown creased Felipe's forehead. 'Running away is something you do rather well, isn't it?'

Evie flushed.

'If I could explain . . . ' she started to speak but Felipe wasn't listening.

'I do not normally pursue women who keep walking out on me, I find it tedious, but for you I am prepared to make an exception.' Evie closed her eyes, hoping to discourage Felipe from lecturing her further but it did no good. Felipe continued speaking.

'Nancy's poor driver must have found it most tiresome to keep going backwards and forwards to the airport, but now we are both in the same place at the same time and without outside interruption we have to talk.'

Evie remembered only too well the last time they had spoken. Felipe had said he was in love with her. Was she in love with him?

The emotions he aroused in her were different from any others she had known. She had never met anyone like Felipe. He could be kind and considerate but at the same time haughty and unfeeling but Evie knew that life without him would leave her feeling desolate.

No man could ever measure up to him and that she supposed had to be love. Her generous mouth curved into a reluctant smile.

'What have I said now?' There was a note of exasperation in Felipe's voice.

'It's good to see you again, without uncles, grandmothers and long-lost relatives in the background.'

'I'm pleased to hear it,' Felipe acknowledged, his expression also softening. 'I thought maybe the idea of seeing me again might be unpleasant for you.'

'This used to be my father's vineyard.' Evie spoke in a careful voice, steering the conversation away from how she might be feeling at the sight of Felipe.

'And when he lost it because of the

Vicentes' profligacy he was naturally angry.'

'I knew the Quintas had history with your family,' Evie attempted to explain, 'but my parents would never talk about it. All I wanted to do was find out what happened. When Astra approached Lesli with a view to cataloguing her fashion collection it seemed too good a chance to pass up. Then things started happening.'

'Things?'

'You making me sign a contract, Carlos asking me out, Eduardo being . . . ' she shrugged, 'Eduardo, then Astra was unwell and,' she lowered her eyes wishing Felipe would not look at her quite so intently, 'you know the rest.'

'You do seem to have packed a lot into your stay at the castelo,' Felipe acknowledged.

The waiter delivered Felipe's drink to their table.

'Do you mind if I help myself to some of your nuts?' he asked. 'I don't think I've eaten today.'

'I forgot!' Evie put a horrified hand to her mouth. 'The auction. How did it go?'

'It exceeded all expectations.'

'But now you won't need the funds to renovate the castelo, will you?'

Felipe savoured some of his wine before speaking.

'You mean now that I am no longer the heir? But then I never was, was I?'

'I don't know how much Catherine told you about our conversation.'

'She told me nothing. It was Nancy who provided the missing links in the chain. She read about the auction in a glossy magazine. An enterprising journalist had discovered my connection to Astra and published my photo.'

'And she noticed your resemblance to her son Shaun.'

Felipe nodded.

'So I believe.'

'When did you speak to Nancy?'

'After you left. She accosted me in the foyer and she is not an easy lady to ignore.'

'And?' Evie prompted.

'It was difficult for her to admit she was in the wrong. I admire her for that.'

'What did she do that put her in the wrong?'

'It all goes back to the night of her midsummer birthday party. Everyone assumed Astra's absence was because Shaun's parents did not approve of her background and she had faked a convenient illness rather than face them.'

'Ducking out of things wasn't Astra's style,' Evie put in.

'Exactly. She wasn't unwell but she was in the early stages of pregnancy.'

'I see.'

'Shaun told his parents. Nancy said she would not sanction any marriage between them.'

'But she was too late?'

Felipe nodded.

'They were already married. You are not surprised?' He raised his eyebrows.

'I found your mother's birth certificate hidden in the lining of Astra's black and white checked coat. Cassandra's mother's name was given as Astra Merrony, formerly Backshaw.'

A wry smile twisted Felipe's mouth. 'You knew about Aggie Backshaw?'

'Astra told me,' Evie admitted. 'She also told me her father was a miner and her mother worked in a shop.'

'Then you can imagine how that went down with Nancy and Eugene Merrony.'

'They weren't best pleased?'

'There was a big argument and Shaun stormed out of the party after telling them he preferred his wife's company to that of his narrow-minded parents. Those were his exact words.'

'Poor Nancy.'

'His father wanted to go after him but Nancy held him back saying Shaun needed time to cool off.'

'And that's what he did in the swimming pool?'

'So it would seem.'

'What a sad story.'

'Astra fled to Portugal. Eugene and Nancy had no idea where she had gone and soon after that Eugene Merrony was posted back to Washington and that phase of their life came to a close.'

'And Astra never told them about Cassandra?'

'No.'

'What about Mauricio?'

'Astra was heartbroken over losing the love of her life. Mauricio was, I suppose, looking for someone to love. Antonio was his father's favourite son.'

'Did you ever think Mauricio might not be your natural grandfather?'

There was a faraway look in Felipe's eyes.

'I always suspected something. I think Eduardo did too. He assumed, wrongly, that Mauricio and Astra weren't married.'

'I wonder why your grandmother never told you about Shaun.'

'Who knows? Perhaps she thought it would damage our relationship.'

'Does this mean you will be handing over the castelo to Eduardo?' Evie asked.

'It is rightfully his. I would probably have let him live there anyway even if the past hadn't come back to haunt us. I have no emotional attachment to it.'

'I have to admit I hid behind a pillar to avoid Eduardo outside the auction house.'

'You need never see him again,' Felipe assured her.

'He wanted me to go through your grandmother's things to see if I could find any evidence to support his claim to the castelo.'

'What sort of evidence?'

'I don't know. I told him I couldn't find something that wasn't there. I mean, if Mauricio and Astra hadn't been married then they wouldn't have had a marriage certificate.'

'He was, I think, desperate.' Felipe spoke slowly. 'Like his father he has mounting debts. He will probably try to sell the castelo.'

'What will you do now?' Evie asked.

'I think I'd like to go for a walk along the harbour. It is beautiful at this time of night. Will you join me?'

Although Evie's question had not been about Felipe's immediate future she was glad he appeared to have misunderstood her. 'You can leave your holdall here. We'll come back for it later.'

Marina was typical of many small fishing communities on the southern-most tip of the country. It did not hold the attraction of the fashionable resorts being too small and tucked away in a small inlet dominated by the rugged coastline of the old mediaeval fortress.

Evie stood by the water's edge inhaling the aroma of the sea while Felipe had a few words with some of the fishermen. Behind her the bou-tiques dotted around the harbour were closing up for the day.

It was still early in the season and it was possible to stroll along the water-front without being jostled by tourists keen to take photos.

'Visitors bring much needed income to the area,' Felipe admitted, 'but there is always a downside to everything. They leave litter. Plastic especially is a severe problem.

'We have to do something to stop the damage man is doing to the natural habitat before it is too late. I have decided to use some of the auction proceeds to set up a foundation in Astra's memory but I can't do it on my own. I need help.'

As they were walking a child pursued by a harassed mother caused Evie to lose her footing. She stumbled but did not fall. It was then she realised Felipe had been holding her hand.

'*Sinto muito*,' the mother apologised as she scooped up the wailing toddler.

'You are all right?' Felipe looked at Evie in concern, 'You did not twist your ankle?'

Evie would have liked to remove her hand from Felipe's but she did not see how she could do so without engaging in an unseemly tussle.

'I'm fine, thank you.'

'Would you like to have children one

day?' Felipe asked.

The question almost caused Evie to lose her footing for a second time.

'I haven't really given the matter much thought,' she admitted.

'I am not like Astra,' Felipe insisted. 'I do not want two secret weddings. I hope to only marry once.' He gave what amounted to a shy smile. 'Have you thought about marriage?'

Evie was glad the evening light hid her blushes.

'I was engaged once,' she admitted.

'What happened?' Felipe asked.

'Things didn't work out,' Evie wished Felipe would change the subject.

'You know how I feel about you,' he said quietly, turning her round to face him. 'We didn't have the best of starts and I admit that was my fault.

'I knew my grandmother had a past and I suppose some of the Vicente pride rubbed off on me. I didn't want the world knowing about her. She had chosen a quiet life and she had the right to privacy.'

'Felipe,' Evie hesitated, 'I'm not sure how I feel about anything right now.'

'You dealt with everything we threw at you didn't you? And more.' Felipe added, 'It can't have been easy.'

'There were times,' Evie admitted, 'when I would have cheerfully torn up your wretched contract.'

'If it is of any consolation Catherine has changed her mind about you. She thinks you would make a good Portuguese wife.'

'Hold on one moment.' Evie could feel the hairs on the back of her neck begin to rise in protest.

'That is good,' Felipe looked as though he were enjoying the exchange. 'You are annoyed.'

'You bet I am. I am not intending to get married to anybody right now, and when I do the relationship will be on an equal basis. If you expect me to run around with your slippers in my hand like a good little wife then you've got another think coming.'

Before Evie could protest further

Felipe crushed her body to his and kissed her.

'What are you doing?' She wriggled free.

'Something I've wanted to do for a long time and trying to convince you that I would make a good husband. How do you feel about plastic?'

'I beg your pardon?'

'And marine life? And the environment?'

'Felipe.' Evie put her hands to her ears.

'Will you be my lifelong partner?'

'All this talk about marriage is unsettling.'

'Are you too modern for an established institution?'

Evie couldn't help smiling.

'You sound like a talking dictionary,' she said, 'and in answer to your question I am not ready for an institution.'

'Then I am wasting my time asking you to marry me?'

'You could try,' Evie said.

'Would you like me to go down on one knee?'

'Not here.' Evie cast a nervous look around the harbour. Several of the fishermen were regarding them with indulgent smiles.

'All right, I agree. It might attract attention.' Felipe drew her back into his arms. Evie could feel his heart beating against hers. 'I do not think marriage to me would be a walk in the park. I can be,' he hesitated, 'I think the expression is tricky?'

'Really?' Evie feigned surprise.

'Yes, really,' Felipe insisted, before he realised Evie was teasing him. 'Do you accept my proposal?'

The expression in his eyes was enough to convince Evie that whatever the future held for them, Felipe was her destiny.

'I do,' she said in a soft voice.

'Hey,' one of the fishermen called to his mate, 'Felipe has just got engaged to his English girlfriend.'

'Have they got radar?' Evie demanded looking round at the sea of smiling faces.

'Perhaps, or perhaps they recognise

the face of a man in love when they see one.'

'I never had you down as a sentimentalist,' Evie chided.

'I can be all sorts of things,' Felipe insisted. 'Why don't I show you?'

'That sounds like a good idea.'

They remained silhouetted on the harbour as a light mist rolled in from the sea and the fishermen packed up their crates.

FESTIVAL FEVER
LOVE WILL FIND A WAY
HUNGRY FOR LOVE
ISLAND MAGIC
THE EIGHTH CHILD

We do hope that you have enjoyed reading this large print book.

Did you know that all of our titles are available for purchase?

We publish a wide range of high quality large print books including:
Romances, Mysteries, Classics
General Fiction
Non Fiction and Westerns

Special interest titles available in large print are:
The Little Oxford Dictionary
Music Book, Song Book
Hymn Book, Service Book

Also available from us courtesy of Oxford University Press:
Young Readers' Dictionary
(large print edition)
Young Readers' Thesaurus
(large print edition)

For further information or a free brochure, please contact us at:
Ulverscroft Large Print Books Ltd.,
The Green, Bradgate Road, Anstey,
Leicester, LE7 7FU, England.
Tel: (00 44) **0116 236 4325**
Fax: (00 44) **0116 234 0205**